burning
from
the
inside

ch
wa

D

**Canada Council
for the Arts** **Conseil des Arts
du Canada**

The publisher gratefully acknowledges the support of the Canada Council for the
Arts and the Ontario Arts Council for its publishing program. We acknowledge the
financial support of the Government of Canada through the Canada Book Fund
(CBF) for our publishing activities, and the Government of Ontario through the
Ontario Media Development Corporation, an agency of the Ontario Ministry of
Culture, and the Ontario Book Publishing Tax Credit Program.

LIBRARY AND ARCHIVES CANADA CATALOGUING IN PUBLICATION

Walde, Christine, 1969–
Burning from the inside / Christine Walde.

Issued also in electronic formats.
ISBN 978-1-77086-246-3

1. Title.

PS8645.A456B87 2013   jC813'.6   C2013-900481-5

Cover art and design: Angel Guerra/Archetype
Interior text design: Tannice Goddard, Soul Oasis Networking
Printer: Friesens

Printed and bound in Canada.

The interior of this book is printed on 100% post-consumer waste recycled paper.

DANCING CAT BOOKS
An imprint of Cormorant Books Inc.
390 Steelcase Road East, Markham, Ontario, L3R 1G2
www.cormorantbooks.com

for those who know how it feels

Let age and sickness silent rob
The vineyards in the night;
But those who burn with vig'rous youth
Pluck fruits before the light.

— William Blake, from
"Are Not the Joys of Morning Sweeter"

We climbed and we climbed
Oh, how we climbed
...
Over the stars
To the top of Tiger Mountain

— Brian Eno, from "Taking Tiger Mountain"

Graffiti equals amazing to me.

— Banksy

I.

Remember me. That's all a tag says, no matter how big or small, he thinks. A way of saying I was here. I matter. I am not invisible. Since time began. Like those caves in Lascaux, France. Ages old. Prehistoric graffito.

He has his favourite tags. Lately it's been the pizza slice. He's seen it bombed all over the city: high up on rooftops, on hard-to-reach billboards, fire escapes. On overpasses. Underpasses. Train bridges.

It was nothing but a triangle on its side with a double strip of lines on the left for the crust; circles in the middle for the pepperoni. "The Pizza Dude": that's what everyone was calling him. Of course no one knew who he was. But that's the way it is. The way it's supposed to be. You are your tag. That is your identity.

There's something fresh and pure about the smell of paint, he thinks. How it's clean and new, like snow. And this is what he imagines as he writes, like he's laying something down, changing the shape of things, creating a new curve, a new drift. A new landscape.

He shakes the can, bending down along the wall, steadily moving his hand right in the light of his headlamp, following the curve of the line. He takes a quick peek over his shoulder. Looks into the dark of the park. Just to see if anyone's out there. Watching. Only the limbs of the trees move, shifting their branches, swaying in the warm, dark wind.

He turns back to the wall and keeps spraying. He can't remember how many tags he's done tonight. He started just after dark at the other end of the city, winding his way along the river trail to downtown. He will keep going all night, ending at the other end of the city where the trail loops around. Then he will sleep. Then, and only then.

He is almost finished. He works quickly, adding the last touches. Close by, a train rumbles past, barrelling along the rails. The sound is deafening. *Concentrate*, he tells himself, *concentrate*. The train whistles, and his hand slips, the line blurring. He breathes slowly, quietly. Peering at his work. He will have to do it again. *Damn it.*

He takes another spray can out of his backpack. Stops. Thinks he hears something. Turns his headlamp off. Peers out into the darkness again. Some people shout and leap through the park, running toward the playground. He watches them: six bodies charging the swings, standing up and pulling the ropes back, bending their bodies into the air.

For a moment he forgets himself, watching them. Under the streetlamps the insects swarm, points of diamond light, buzzing, brilliant white. He watches them, mesmerized, like they're hundreds of matches flaring into flame, one by one. The train is now gone. Distant in his ear, his mind, his memory. The moon a dirty pearl hanging in the dark green sea of the night.

He turns back to the cement wall and studies the tag half-heartedly in the shadows. Afraid to see the work he's done. The mistakes he knows he's made. He turns his headlamp on and looks carefully, seeing where the fuzzy blue fragmentary cusp of spray paint bends and arcs like a ring around a distant planet. It doesn't look that bad, he decides. It's not his best work, but it is *his*. And he's tagged more than anyone in this city. King under the mountain.

In the background, the people on the swings whoop and holler, then stop. Like an animal, he freezes. Smelling the air. The quick silence. His neck pricks with fear. *Shit.* Headlights swerve over the back of his head, hot and white. In one movement he turns his headlamp off and throws his bag aside and drops down on his belly. Burying his head in the ground cover. His breathing stuttered, panicky. *Don't move*, he thinks. *Don't make a sound.* He feels the headlights sweep and burn over his back, searching into the darkness of the park, scanning the wall. *Fuckfuckfuck*, he thinks. Screaming the words aloud in his brain. Not daring to flinch. Then the lights go out.

He waits for what feels like a thousand lifetimes. Listening to the river below him, rushing by in a cool gurgle. Then, slowly, carefully, he inches his way along the ground, toward the riverbank, his head still down, hidden from view. His heart pounding so hard he's glad he doesn't have to stand because he's sure his legs won't hold him. He was told the next time he got caught there'd be no pardon, no privileges. He can hardly breathe for the fear he feels choking him. *That was close.*

At the edge of the riverbank, he raises his head and looks up into the darkness. Sees the river trail by the colour of night, now dark blue, leaning toward dawn. His disappointment like a weight he feels in his arms, sad and heavy. He will not be doing any more graff tonight. He pulls himself up on his haunches and crouches by the river's edge. Wishes he had something to drink. Then he remembers his bag. He looks up to where he once was, under the bridge. *It's been long enough now.*

He scales the ground cover with his hands, searching for his bag, finding it where he had ditched it last. As he grabs the shoulder straps, his hands ignite under bright, white light.

He tries to roll away, but it is too late. He hears a voice: a man's, slow, plodding, authoritative. Telling him to stand up. To put his hands up. To turn around and stand before the light. The hot beams burn through his clothes on his back.

He knows the drill. He doesn't get to ask questions. He just does what he's told and turns around, bowing his head, shielding his eyes from the light.

II.

It always begins with the sound of a train. I can hear it coming at me through the darkness of my dream — the low, distant rumble echoing through what I can and cannot see. As it gets closer, the sound gets louder in my ears. Wheels grinding over steel, ringing, clattering over the rails. That's when I can smell it. The sharp stink of metal and sulphur. And that's when I know that she's going to be there, waiting for me.

Story.

I had the dream about Story last night. Again. The same dream I always have. First there's the sound of the train. Then I'm walking downtown, and all the buildings are bright and shiny and the sidewalks are gold, and even though it's daytime the stars are all out and the sky sparkles. Everything sparkles.

And all the people walking down the street are beautiful, and not in a movie star kind of way, but deep down inside, right to the core of their soul, like they're naked on the outside, wholly and completely loved for who they are. Unconditionally.

And I'm there too, and all I can think about is how I can't believe that this is the city where I live and all the closed-up shops are open and full of light and all the freaks and junkies are like angels with wings and it's lightly cool like after a summer rain and everything feels new and clean and rainbows are bursting everywhere.

And then I see Story. She's always standing there, in the middle of the street, waiting for me, her hands in her pockets, a wise, wide smile on her face, mischief in her eyes. She reaches out and takes my hand and it's lightly cool, too, just like the rain, and then she always says: *I've been waiting for you.* And then I always say: *I've been waiting for you, too.* And that's when I feel like my guts are going to burst because she smiles this smile at me again and we turn around and walk hand in hand down the shiny golden streets of the town toward where I know The Ten will be, where she will, at last, show me her last great masterpiece.

She who is so familiar and yet a total stranger, whose work I have come to know most intimately and so completely and yet who I will never, ever meet. How is it that our lives are so completely and fantastically intertwined in this dream I always have? This dream that always ends the same way: I ask her where The Ten are and she turns to me and says, *Look back.* And I turn my head to see what she sees and she says, *Don't you see?*

And before I know it she's gone. Disappeared completely. And I'm standing alone in the street again, and it's the same as it always was, with all the shitty abandoned storefronts and homeless people and head shops and tattoo parlours and everyone's waiting for a bus to take them somewhere and The Ten are nowhere in sight.

And that's when I wake up, knowing that I have to keep looking for them, knowing that they're somewhere in this city and not just in my dreams, but real, down some darkened street, along the Kalpa Path, on the top of Tiger Mountain, waiting for me to find them.

III.

Thom walked nervously down the narrow hallway of the first floor of the youth correctional services building. He read the name on the business card that had been given to him by the guard: E.B. O'Brien, Investigations Manager, Youth Correctional Services. Room 101.

Thom knocked. A man wearing a dark blue suit and tie, who was standing talking on the phone, opened the door and waved him into the room, directing him toward a chair in front of his desk. As he held the receiver to his ear, O'Brien coolly surveyed Thom, nodding his head.

Uh-huh. Yeah. He's right here. In my office. Uh-huh.

O'Brien looked at Thom again and continued to talk into the phone.

Like I said, he's here now. I'll update you later. O'Brien hung up and sat down at his desk, studying Thom. So. Got caught again, did we? What is it this time? Your third offence?

Thom looked away from O'Brien's stare and shrugged again, saying nothing. He stared at the wall, studying O'Brien's degrees and his certificates of honour, looking at the obligatory pictures of his wife and family.

O'Brien reached for a single manila folder from the stack on his desk. He flipped it open and skimmed over the surface of the pages, studying their small black type.

Says here, O'Brien said, you first got picked up in '08. In La belle province. Montreal. Then again in '09. This time, Ottawa. And once before. In T.O. Just a mere six weeks ago. All the same stuff: violation of public property. *Graff.*

O'Brien's use of the term annoyed Thom. O'Brien continued:

Says you also go by a number of different names. So-called *tags*. Including, but not limited to — O'Brien emphasized the words that were written before him — Alpha, Byte, Byron, Creep, DNA, Doom, Kid A, Kubla Khan, Maximus, Neo, Nexxxus, Oracle, Omega ...

As O'Brien went through the list, Thom listened to each name, each identity he had owned or possessed, even for just an hour or a day. He'd done it for no other reason than because he wanted to. Like switching up an old set of clothes for something new. But how, Thom wondered, had they known that they were all *him*? Had they really been following him all these years?

O'Brien continued reading from the list: ... UFO, Waldo, and ZZZ. At least that's what we know about. To name a few.

O'Brien tossed the folder back onto his desk and leaned back in his chair.

So why do you do it?

Thom stared at the black holster under O'Brien's arm. He might be wearing a suit and tie and have a desk job, Thom thought, but he's still a cop.

Thom shrugged once more, looking down.

You can quit the dumb act with me. The IQ test you took shows you're way off the chart. So don't think I don't know what you're trying to pull.

Thom looked defiantly at O'Brien.

You wouldn't understand, Thom said finally.

Don't presume to know I don't understand anything that you've been through, he replied. He smiled tersely. But I'm not the one breaking the law.

O'Brien waited for Thom's reaction, but Thom just stared back at O'Brien.

Why am I here?

O'Brien stood up and looked out the window.

Have you ever heard of the G7?

Thom shook his head. No.

Good, O'Brien said. Because that means they probably haven't heard of you either. Yet.

What are you talking about? Thom asked.

Your ticket out. We want you to help us crack a crew called the G7.

Thom burst out laughing.

No way, man. I work alone. I'd rather do time than be a rat for you and take down a group of fellow writers. Get fucking real.

O'Brien turned around and stared Thom down.

Your real name is Thomas. Nash. Taylor. The fifth. Born in Montreal. Raised in various cities, including New York, London, Ottawa. Son of some diplomat. Nothing but the best private school education. But you ran away from home in 2009 when you were fifteen. Been on the street ever since.

Thom cringed. He hated hearing his name in full. Everything about it, from its tradition to the expectation that he would carry it on into the future, filled him with hate. He grimaced while O'Brien moved away from the window and walked around Thom.

Your parents have been looking for you, but you're nowhere to be found. And the detectives they've hired haven't been much help. They don't know how to play your game. How to find your name, locate your tag, your territory. And when you crossed the border to go stateside in 2010 they thought they might have caught you, but it was too late. You were gone again. Completely vanished. No trace. They didn't even know where to start to look. But by then you were already someone else. And you've been MIA ever since. Well, at least 'til now.

O'Brien paused and sat back down at his desk and faced Thom, cracking a hardened smile.

You sure don't want to be found, do you?

Thom kept his eyes steady on O'Brien but said nothing.

In fact, O'Brien continued, it seems you'd rather let us find you than them. And since I've learned from HQ that you've acted as an informant before to save your ass from being found by your folks, I'm betting that you're willing to do it again. Except this time you're going to go underground. Undercover. For us. We have some information, but it's not much. The rest will be up to you. For your efforts, we'll give you a clean record. So squeaky you'll think you're wearing a new goddamn pair of shoes.

No fucking way, Thom said.

O'Brien weighed Thom's response with a tired compliance. I bet you think you've seen me, or cops like me, in the movies, right?

O'Brien reached for the telephone and began pressing a series of numbers.

Then you'll know exactly how this works. Just like in the movies. I begin by putting in a call to our people.

O'Brien put the phone to his ear.

Yeah, it's me. Could you get me the contact info for the private detective handling the Taylor case? Yeah. Yeah. Thanks.

Thom glared at O'Brien as panic rushed to his chest.

You're bullshitting, Thom said.

O'Brien grabbed the bottom end of the receiver and swung it away from his mouth. No, he mouthed, as he smiled at Thom and reached for a pen and notepad.

Yeah, I'm still here, he said. What's that? You can connect me directly? Perfect.

Thom stared at O'Brien's steely grey hair. His large, ruddy hands. The coarse stubble on his chin. Hate throbbed in his head.

Uh, yeah, good morning. O'Brien here. I was wondering if I could speak to Detective Smith? Yes, I'll hold.

Thom sat in the chair and clenched his fist. Whatever happened, he couldn't go back home.

Thom leaned forward and pulled the phone away from O'Brien's ear and hung it up.

O'Brien looked up at Thom and smiled. See? Just like in the movies.

IV.

Went to the Bridge tonight to celebrate us. The one and only G7. Danced my face off. Blissfully drunk on some tequila Chef BS brought just for the occasion. The bottle being passed around freely as we each took a mouthful, gulping it back in chugs. Foregoing the lemon, the salt. Just the pure hallucinatory elixir of agave. Feeling like I was floating as we celebrated the news today about our last little staging in the parking lot of the Woodland Mall. Chef's idea, of course. An abandoned vehicle left under the lights with a dummy Grim Reaper inside, *Consumerism Kills* spray-painted on the side panel doors. Shopping bags bursting out the back seat.

According to the late-night security guard, she didn't see anything until all the other cars had left. And nothing showed up on the security cameras. It was like it simply appeared out of thin air, she was quoted as saying.

Such a sweet piece. One of our best yet. But, apparently, the 5-0 were not impressed. They mentioned in the press that whoever had done this was also responsible for some of the other "singularly unique protest pranks" that had been taking place over the past few months, including the rash of recent protest graffiti throughout the city, as well as the flash mob in front of the downtown branch of the Dominion Securities Commission.

Sometimes I still wonder if we're ever going to get caught. But Chef BS had said that wasn't ever going to happen. We were safe, he said. Protected. He'd made sure of that. And all of us knew better than to question him. His word.

The DC making eyes at me tonight. As if we could just get back together again for one more night, one more sweet embrace. Me batting my eyes, giving it all I had, dancing with MC Lee, gyrating all crazy-like against her while DJ O'd played. As if I could. I knew The Rule. I could be excommunicated because of our little romantic entanglement. Short and sweet as it was. His soft kisses. The melting wall of his tongue.

Chef watched me from his usual table, enjoying me and MC Lee dancing. Kane silent beside him, Queen Mab beside him. Another cute boy across the dance floor trying to dance with me and MC Lee. Probably wanting some threesome. MC Lee doing all her usual magic. Both of us playing out his adolescent fantasy. Him calling his other friends over to watch us dance together. So much fun. But at the end of the night he wanted to take it all home. Make it real. As if. MC Lee and I trying to shoo the poor puppy home. But alas he just would not leave it alone. Or us. Tsk tsk. Well by then Kane just had to step in. Nothing like a giant of a man to set a poor sod straight. Queen Mab and Chef watched from the sidelines, just in case.

What I want to know is why can't a girl just dance? That's what I want. I want someone to just watch me dance and not want me for my body but for what my soul is saying. I want someone to want me in that way: the absolute magic of soul-bending love. The spark of that. Setting me on fire. Pure. True. Love like no other: the ether of desire.

Tired now. Must sleep. Thanks to Queen Mab, we've all got jobs at the Ridgeway Country Club. Starting tomorrow morning. School's over for now but I think I can serve up some revolution with a smile.

May I take your order, please?

V.

Thom studied O'Brien sitting in the seat across from him on the train. He'd lost the tie but still had the suit jacket and the holster. Thom had spent the better part of two weeks with O'Brien, learning about the G7, about what he was going to do, his *modus operandi*.

Thom shifted in his seat in his new clothes, running his hand through his new haircut, looking at his new shoes — the uniform he had been designated to wear, all expenses paid. He even had a new name. TNT. It had been O'Brien's idea, a way of getting up, as he said, with a bang. The fact that O'Brien had selected the initials of his full name as his new tag did not go unnoticed by him.

Thom looked outside the window, into fields of rolling green and vistas of blue sky. The rattling lull of the train bored into Thom's brain, making him feel queasy. He wasn't used to being this new person. But he knew he'd have to grow into it, into his new identity. Really, he had no choice. This was who he had to be now.

During his time with O'Brien, Thom had been under constant police escort, and now he was about to be set free, into an unknown scene, into an unknown city. Thom had already decided he'd just do the work he needed to do and then get his exit pass. He could probably get the information O'Brien needed in a couple of weeks. Then he would be free again.

Thom looked out the window again. They were entering the city. At first, the graffiti was largely average: amateurs with a paint marker, writing out some tag they'd designed in their bedroom. He saw the names of other writers, too, emerging out of the landscape: Oscar, Fade, Pmon.

Then Thom saw a life-size stencil of blacked-out people holding balloons in neon pink, hot yellow, and orange marked with nuclear radiation symbols, gas masks over their faces. Further on, there were colossal stencils of piles of dollar bills with an arrow beside them saying *Free Money*. Still further on, skulls on flower stems across an entire section of fencing. And then, a stencil of a man and woman and two children holding hands under a blazing sun. Under them, the message *Every Day Is a Beautiful Day Thanks to Global Warming*.

Thom could feel O'Brien watching him, studying his reaction.

That, said O'Brien, is the work of the G7.

Thom looked at their designs as they sped past. Once upon a time, they had probably been seen as little more than an annoyance, Thom thought, a group of kids getting their kicks with a can of spray. But as they gained more confidence, they had taken more risks in terms of size and scale, testing their limits — and subject matter — as a crew.

What do you think? O'Brien asked.

Def, said Thom.

Too bad the taxpayers and property owners don't feel the same way, O'Brien scoffed. Do you know how much it costs to clean this shit up?

Thom held O'Brien's gaze. Maybe if they could just see it the way I do they wouldn't feel that way.

They disappeared through the darkness of an underpass and emerged into a concrete landscape of flat, featureless grey. Thom looked out the window and saw tag after tag erased, entire walls of graffiti covered over with grey paint.

What the fuck is this? Thom asked.

A couple of years back, O'Brien said, this city passed legislation restricting the sale of cans of spray paint and paint markers to youth under the age of eighteen. City council passed the bylaw because they felt it could quell the graffiti activity in the city and reduce incidents of vandalism. O'Brien paused. As you can see, it hasn't been entirely successful.

Obviously, Thom said bluntly.

And what I didn't tell you, or what I couldn't tell you until now, is what you'll be doing when you're not acting on our behalf. Under the terms of your sentence you have to provide a community service. Rehabilitation, they call it. Yours will be cleaning up graffiti.

What? Thom exclaimed. *Buffing*? He felt sick to his stomach.

Don't worry, O'Brien said. You'll still get to write at night. All you want. Wherever you want. And you'll be protected by our people. So you won't ever have to worry about getting caught. But in exchange I want real information. Names, addresses. I don't want to be chasing ghosts.

For a moment, Thom imagined the freedom that could come with not having to worry about getting caught, creating mind-blowing tags and stencils and murals that defied any prior scope or proportion. Then he imagined having to eliminate them, destroying what he had created. His masterpieces reduced to a flat field of grey.

Thom looked hard at O'Brien. What you really mean is you want me to *erase* it. *Censor* my own fucking work —

Thom couldn't finish his sentence; he listened to the tragic note of his own voice trail off into the air.

You can call it "work" if you want, O'Brien answered, but it's against the law. You still have to undo it. O'Brien paused. Winston can help you out with any other questions you have. He's our man in the field. Your contact. And mine. He's meeting us at the station where he'll escort you to the detention complex we've got set up for guys like you. It's by the river, downtown, in a prime location. It's not a total lockdown facility, but there's twenty-four-hour surveillance. Because of the work you'll be doing for us, you'll have special status. No curfew. When you're not working, that is. No one else will know about the reason for your presence there but Winston. And you will report to me only. Is that clear? He paused. Winston will debrief you on everything else when you arrive.

Thom stared out the window again. They were nearing downtown and once again the streets and alleyways and buildings were covered with graff. This time in red and black and white. Against a forest of trees, Thom saw a large stencil of a computer screen that said *Log Off*. Immediately he understood that no information O'Brien had told him could have prepared him for what he was about to do.

And do not, under any circumstances, reveal your true identity, O'Brien said.

VI.

Today was my third day waiting tables at the Ridgeway. All afternoon I felt like screaming out into the dining room: *Shazam! Here I am, your friendly neighbourhood activist, culture-jamming server girl!* All the trophy wives with their perfect dye jobs in their tight t-shirts and white shorts, showing off their new boob jobs and carefully sipping their club sodas, nibbling at their organic green salads. Their emotionless Botox-filled faces lifted tightly away from their eyes like sails in a strong wind. Their whitened teeth smiling, smiling, smiling. Oh the lives of the rich and famous! The beautiful people! Ugh.

The men driving a parade of gleaming SUVs into the parking

lot, jostling and haranguing their buddies in a light beer–
induced buzz while trying to impress their corporate clients,
rolling into the clubhouse to check out this year's seasonal
offering of T&A. Queen Mab and MC Lee and I provocatively
leaning to place the plates of calamari on the table, our hands
gripping the stems of cold, sudsy beers. The wives glinting at
us with jealous, mascara-laden eyes, hating our perfect skin
and flat stomachs. I can almost hear the wheels in their brains
turning, thinking, *If only I could have that, now. What I could get!*
And us in the kitchen, doing shooters in the walk-in cooler.
Watching DJ O'dysseus on the line and The DC behind the grill.
Knives wielded, furiously chopping. Kane out on the course,
of course. Cutting grass, smoking grass. Cleaning the pool.
Scrubbing the courts.

Sigh. What a summer this was going to be.

Pulled in a whack-o-cash in tips last night. Enough to make
my parents happy this morning and not ask what I'm doing
with my summer. If they only knew. If they only cared. My father
checking his email and my mother texting at the kitchen table
this morning. Drinking their Starbucks coffee. Both of them
lost in another world. My brother boorish on his Nintendo, listening to his iPod, shovelling puffs of crunchy-but-unnameable-
Styrofoam-like cereal into his mouth with no-doubt-laden-with-
growth-hormones milk before being shipped off to summer
camp. All of them slaves to technology. Data drones, vacuously
drowning, one touch screen away from death. I mean, I love
them dearly. But really. Seriously. They need help.

Queen Mab read me my cards today. Her tiny hands placing
the cards on my bed, turning them over. Telling me that there
is some auspicious movement in the universe or something.
A stranger. Aligning toward my astral position. Some potent
force. Maybe a magic boy? Just for me? Oooh, goody-goody, I

said. Clapping my hands. Then Queen Mab said the weirdest thing: she couldn't read the cards into the future. As if there was a strange cosmic uncertainty. Gee, no shit, I replied. Queen Mab said it wasn't funny, getting all weird and mystical on me, saying something truly profoundly life-changing is going to happen to me. Real soon. I just have to be aware of my surroundings. To listen. And watch for the sign.

Then I asked her if she could tell me what it was, and she couldn't determine what it was other than some kind of flame. A fire. Some kind of explosion. Whatever that means.

All I know is that I'm waiting. And my eyes are wide open.

VII.

When Thom and O'Brien got off the platform at the train station, Winston was waiting for them. He was an unassuming man of average size, wearing jeans and a grey t-shirt, mirrored sunglasses covering his eyes, and a ball cap on his head, his long greying hair tied in a loose ponytail. Thom watched closely as the two men shook hands with a polite, businesslike acrimony.

This is Winston, O'Brien said to Thom.

Winston looked at Thom, studying him disapprovingly. He turned to O'Brien.

This is him? Are you sure you want to go ahead with this? he asked. Like I already told you, if you're looking for information, I've already got contacts on the ground, in the field, ready to go.

There was a moment of uncomfortable silence. O'Brien looked at Winston and motioned him impatiently aside. Thom stood there, watching, as the two of them talked low and quietly. He didn't have to try to make out what they were saying: he knew right away he wasn't wanted. It was O'Brien's operation and Thom was crashing in on Winston's turf, and, not surprisingly, Winston was not impressed that he had to babysit him.

O'Brien and Winston turned around and walked toward him.

I hear we're going to be working together, Winston said uncomfortably. Good to meet you.

Thom nodded, staring at his reflection mirrored in Winston's sunglasses. He hardly recognized himself.

Yeah, Thom replied, unsure. Good to meet you, too.

In the car they were mostly silent. Winston drove while O'Brien went through some papers in his briefcase. Thom stared out the window, taking in the new city he would call home.

He could tell that at one point in its history, it had been a wealthy and prosperous middle-class town. But now the five-and six-storey buildings that lined the main streets of downtown were crumbling and in a state of disrepair. At street level, there was a mishmash of variety stores, coffee shops, pawn shops, tattoo parlours, and head shops, accented by a few gourmet restaurants, jewellers, and used bookstores. But all the other storefronts were either empty or closed. People in business suits walked past panhandlers begging along the dirty sidewalks — dejected, paranoid, and poor — while the buses roared past, clogged at every junction. Like most small cities of its size, it had succumbed to the disease of urban sprawl. It was like a body without a heart: all the blood and money of the centre rushing to the fingertips where the malls and suburbs were, leaving the major organs to carry the burden of the city's suffering. Not surprisingly, graffiti was everywhere.

Just outside the downtown core, Winston drove the car across a bridge. Outside the window, Thom saw a huge concrete embankment leading down to a river and a system of parks lined with asphalt paths. Further downriver, he could see a number of bridges connecting one side of the city with the other. As he was looking at the small, modest houses dotting the streets, Winston pulled over into a shaded parking lot. Thom looked behind him. The sign outside only said 70 Riverside Drive.

This is it, Winston said to Thom. Your new home away from home: the Riverside Youth Detention and Rehabilitation Centre. Or the Ryder, as all the guys here call it.

Thom stared disappointedly out the car window at the grey, two-level concrete building, all its windows closed, the drapes drawn shut. From one of the windows he saw the single solitary face of a guy with short black hair and piercing black eyes.

It looks just like a juvie, Thom thought as he got out of the car and followed Winston and O'Brien. Or a rehab. Fucking great.

As they approached the rear door, he could see a camera above, enclosed in a protective metal cage. As Winston punched in a security code to open the door, and it buzzed open, Thom felt the truth of his situation hit him straight between the eyes. It wasn't jail, but it might as well have been.

Inside the centre, Thom walked between O'Brien and Winston, shuffling past open doorways into narrow rooms decorated with single beds and desks and dressers, all in matching gun-metal grey. A smell of burnt toast pervaded the air, mixed with stale sweat and floor cleaner. Under the humming drone of the fluorescent lights, on the walls were posters advertising help lines, job and volunteer opportunities, as well as a series of motivational mountain posters saying things like *It is not the mountain we conquer but ourselves, Doubt makes the mountain that faith can move,* and *The man who removes the mountain begins by carrying away small stones.* As they walked further down, an impish guy with dreadlocks came bounding down the hallway, grinning, looking at all of them.

Hey, is this a new brohah? he shouted, looking at Thom.

Yes, Jeremy, Winston answered.

Dunzo. Welcome to the Ryder, dude, Jeremy said to Thom, giving him a hang loose sign.

Thom watched as O'Brien gave Winston a suspicious sideways glance. As they passed another room, Thom saw a guy with pale, coffee-coloured skin and tattoos sitting in a chair in his room, reading. It was the same guy Thom had seen looking out the window. Except now he was wearing big thick black reading glasses.

Hey, Carlos, Winston said.

Carlos raised his head from his book to look at Winston. He stared at Thom, unsmiling.

What are you reading now? asked Winston.

Carlos flipped over the cover of the book for them to see: 1984.

One of the finest volumes from my library, Winston said.

Carlos nodded and then looked back down at the pages in front of him.

Thom continued to follow Winston and O'Brien down the hall, wondering when he would get to his room. Thom wanted nothing more than to sit down and close the door and escape into the privacy of his own thoughts, to plan what he needed to do.

They turned a corner and entered a kitchen area where there were mismatched tables and chairs on one side, and a television and a couple of sagging couches on the other. On the surrounding walls were more mountain posters. In front of the kitchen counter were three guys gathered around a toaster, with their backs turned, bemoaning their breakfast.

Yo, you said you was gonna toast the bread, not burn it, man, said the largest of the three.

I don't give a damn. Where's the jam, man? said the second largest. I like it black.

This made the third one, the smallest, and the first one, the largest, laugh hysterically.

We know you like it black, man, said the third.

Yeah, you like it black, all right. All night long, said the first.

Helplessly, the second one began to laugh too, his shoulders rotating in waves of laughter. Then, sensing someone else was in the room, the third one turned around. Then the second, then the first. Their smiles gone.

The largest of the three looked at Winston, his eyes the colour of iced tea, teeth white as snow.

Yo, Winston. What's up, man?

Nothing much, Winston said. Just wanted to introduce you to our latest Ryder. He's going to be staying with us for a while. This is Tariq, Duke, and Ray.

The three of them looked at Thom and nodded in acknowledgement.

We're just taking him to his room, Winston informed them. He'll be beside you, Duke.

Cool, Duke replied casually. He was the smallest of the three of them.

Thom wasn't sure how to act, who to engage. What to say. He knew he was being judged for everything he was — and wasn't — right now. His clothes, his hair, his skin, his size. In response, Thom just nodded back, playing it safe. He would get his chance, later, to get to know all of them. Find his niche, where he fit in.

Impatiently, O'Brien looked at his watch. Winston stared at him warily, motioning Thom back out into the hallway.

It's just ahead, Winston said. First door on your right.

Thom stepped into the room, leaving O'Brien and Winston, and stared at the single mattress, the bureau, the desk, the chair. Moving forward toward the window, he pulled back the curtain and stared outside the barred glass. The sun blazed fierce and hot, bouncing off the river below, a mesmerizing diamond-like haze glittering upon the surface of the waves. If he was to have any life here, he decided, it would be outside the four walls of this room, out there.

Then Thom remembered the concrete embankment he'd seen by the river; the bridges; the parks. All that space. To move in; to write in. And with no limitations; no restrictions. For the first time, Thom felt his fear diminish. He saw his arrangement with O'Brien as a strange creative freedom he would be allowed to explore. A freedom without risk. Or fear.

So what if he was a rat for O'Brien. He didn't care. He would create so much graffiti that it would be impossible to keep up. Every moment of every night he would create a masterpiece. And then another, and another, and another, until every inch of the city was his, exploding with his name.

Damn right, Thom thought, *I'm TNT.*

VIII.

Just got back from Io. The interplanetary hacienda of Chef BS. His little piece of galaxy by the river and the railroad tracks in the magical forest. I still can't believe how he found that abandoned trailer there. Crazy. Said he was just out early one morning when he saw a tiny silver geometric corner sticking out of the trees. A shape found nowhere in nature, he said. So he went closer and saw there was an abandoned trailer there under the boughs, well-hidden and well-protected. Obviously someone had meant to come back to it, but they never did. Chef picked the lock and opened the door to find a perfectly preserved trailer inside. Said it was just like stepping back in time. Sure, he said, it was a little dusty and moth-eaten, but miraculously clean all the same. So he went and bought a new lock and moved in right away.

Since then he'd decorated it in his own signature style: glow-in-the-dark stars stuck on the ceiling, accented by futuristic silver furniture he'd designed himself, the shelves crammed with books and magazines and vinyl records, all aglow in a sea of blue and white Christmas lights. His chess board taking centre stage, with his hot plate and coffee maker, TV, stereo, and computer hooked up to the singularly powerful solar panel outside. The antenna like a strange beacon to the stars.

He called the trailer Io because it was his inner outer space. Just like the planet. Because that was where he was really from. When he first told me this, he laughed quietly, softly stroking the rust-blond goatee on his chin. His silver eye patch like a mirror, reflecting me back to myself to see. His one good eye a startling blue.

Oh, he's quite the charmer, for sure. That sweet skinny body of his. The soft husky tone of his voice. His mysterious past. I mean, really. It's no wonder Queen Mab has been gaga for him since, like, day one — what little good that is going to do. Even if she is the Queen. She knows The Rule, too. Not that Chef would be interested in anyone. Not since what happened to Story.

Now that it's summer we sit outside by the fire, in our circle of reclaimed chairs Chef has fished out of the river. Surrounding us is his workshop of bicycles and found garbage items. And Kierkegaard, of course — the G7's mascot and faithful canine friend. It was deliriously hot and humid tonight, and we sat sipping cold cans of beer, listening to some satellite radio station from Belgium, planning our next manoeuvres. And us all there, every member of the G7: Chef BS, The DC, the talented DJ O'dysseus, Kane, the fabulous MC Lee, Queen Mab, and me, Aura. The latest and greatest to join their crew.

It's been almost five months now since they caught me tagging on their turf. Casting my Aura around. I had been going it alone, after school, slowly working my way up to bigger tags in more exposed locations. I liked to work with other writers' pre-existing tags, not writing over them exactly, but integrating them into my own piece. My mom and dad were oblivious to what I was doing. They thought it was great. You know, all the "extracurricular time" and "volunteer hours" I was putting in toward the school yearbook.

Oh, sure, I liked to write in all the other usual places: bridges, paths, walkways, underpasses. But big-name corporate billboards were my preferred choice of canvas: the bull's eye of my target. My mission? Nothing less than to alter the stream of society's consciousness by defacing corporate images, dissing on advertising rhythms. All purely political stuff. Kind of a targeted neo-activism, not just throwing down some lame tags so my name gets out there. Whatever. I'm not in it for my ego; I'm in it for altering other people's perceptions. I guess the G7 had been watching me for awhile. Admiring my work. Wanting to know who I was.

Before I joined the G7, the only thing the kids I knew were interested in was how many friends they had, or about some stupid message from someone who didn't care if they were alive or dead, sending texts about what they were going to wear tomorrow. They weren't my friends. They were clones. And I felt like I was disappearing.

The thing that ate away at me was knowing that I was supposed to be in control of it, but I felt powerless. My life didn't mirror what I believed, or what I suspected was happening around me. What I wanted was to feel *real*. Not mediated or controlled through a machine, but in possession of my actual self as I wanted to be represented. In blood and guts and bone. Writing made me feel real.

Story was my first inspiration. I had seen her work around town. And I knew *of* her. But I mean, what writer didn't? She was legendary and kind of impossible to ignore: working up these blockbusters in startling white that would take up the whole side of a building or a wall, on office buildings downtown, in a super-hot white, shaded by black to make the letters pop. And then of course there was The Ten, her epic masterpiece that no one has ever found. At least not yet. As far as anyone knows, The Ten are a set of commandments done in graffiti, taken to be interpreted, quite literally, as a set of truths. Despite this, however, no one has ever found them. So no one quite knows what The Ten are. Except that they exist.

Since I first started looking for them, there have been many rumours about their location. The main one is that the only way to find them is by locating clues along what is known as the Kalpa Path, which leads the way toward Tiger Mountain. Legend has it that Story made the trek to Tiger Mountain every time she learned something that struck her as being a fundamental truth and then wrote it down. Or so I've heard.

Her little stories, however, she left everywhere in public. They were small and quirky, usually no more than three lines, made up of a beginning, a middle, and an end, like this: "Once upon a time a boy and a girl fell in love. Then they fell out of love. They still lived happily ever after." My favourite: "This is the beginning. This is the middle. The End." Her name, of course, signed underneath: *Story*. For a while, they were everywhere. When I was first starting out, her work seemed so different than any of the other graff that was out there. It was fresh, unusual, strange: probably because you could read it, unlike other tags or pieces. In fact, it didn't even seem like graffiti. It was art.

My favourite piece of hers was a stencil of an open book, its pages blank but for a single phrase that said: *What's your story?*

I remember stopping and looking at that piece for a long, long time. I loved how simple and powerful it was — how it made me feel — as if it seemed to be speaking directly to me and no one else, as if someone else understood. That I was out there, and that my story was important, too.

Long before I knew who she was, or about The Ten and what had happened to her, Story inspired me. She made me want to be a writer. And once I started telling my story, I couldn't stop. And then Aura became a part of the landscape, too.

It was Chef who finally tracked me down, of course. I was working up a piece under an overpass one morning, in late winter. It was kind of misty, because all the snow was melting, and I was just standing there in the shadow of a streetlamp tagging when I felt this presence behind me. At first I stood there frozen; I didn't know what to do. Then I started to freak out, because I thought maybe he might have been a DT. When he didn't say anything, I turned around to look and there was this guy standing there with a long black coat on, wearing a black beret and a black eye patch. For a moment I remember thinking *Oh shit, I'm going to die,* because he looked kinda creepy, like Death.

But Chef just smiled this easy, lopsided grin and said (and I never want to forget this until the day I die): So. You are Aura. Your work is beautiful and cunning and true. And so are you. How do you do? My name is Chef BS and I've come to save your soul from the teenage wasteland of your youth.

I remember thinking that he was either totally crazy or a beautiful fucking genius. What I've discovered since is that he is both. Tonight he once again proved his mettle as poet and prophet, father, brother. King.

The G7 really is his baby, his invention. And no one, not even Mab, knows Chef's real name. Where he came from. Or what his story is. No one's even sure how he got the name Chef BS, though Kane said something once about how he was always cooking up bullshit. Apparently he lost his eye when he was a kid, though he never says anything about it other than because he's only got one eye, everything comes to him in a vision. You don't always need eyes to see, comrade Aura, he once told me. He is guided, he says. Shown. Which is his mystique, I guess. That he can "see" things with only one eye.

So, whatever he says is what we do. In return, he protects us. Because the 5-0 are always watching us, getting ready to target us, to take us down.

IX.

Thom's first night at the Ryder, Winston did his best to help him fit in, introducing him to all the guys who were held at the facility. That was the term Winston used: *held*, as if they weren't fully incarcerated, but not totally free, either. In many ways *held* was exactly what they were. As if all of them were in a strange state of suspension between what they had been and what they were supposed to become.

Most of the guys were like him: young vandals, charged with theft, fraud. Some, like Carlos and Jeremy, had been writers, like him. Tariq, Ray, and Duke had been tagging together as a crew and had been caught and convicted together. They were all paying their debt to society, working to clean up graffiti, while working miscellaneous odd jobs. The reason they all lived at the Ryder was that they had nowhere else to go. Winston refused to call it a halfway house because he said there was nothing halfway about it *or* its inhabitants. Apparently there was a two-year waiting list.

The only reason Thom was there was because of his deal with O'Brien. That, and a phony B & E job and public mischief. It was this combination of charges that O'Brien believed would earn him the most respect among the other Ryders and help him gain more information about the G7. And since he was from out of town, and most of the guys at the Ryder were local, there was less chance of Thom — or his work as a writer — being known.

Thom's schedule had been worked out by O'Brien to the last detail: he would do "commserv" — community service — during the day, then "work" at night. Only Winston and O'Brien knew what he would really be doing — writing — before going back to the Ryder to sleep before getting up to buff what he'd bombed the night before.

Back in his room, Thom was unpacking his gear when there was a gentle rap on his door. Panicked, Thom hurriedly closed his suitcase and then went to the door, casually opening it.

In the half-light of the hallway, he met the piercing dark eyes of Carlos, the guy he had seen standing in the window when he first arrived.

I just wanted to tell you, Carlos said as he held up a book, you should check out Winston's library, you know, if you can't sleep. He's got all kinds of crazy shit over there. 'S worth checking out.

Thom raised his face and looked him in the eye.

Thanks.

Carlos stared at him in the light.

It gets better, man, Carlos said. Really. The first night is always the worst.

Thom looked him in the eye. Then looked down again. Thanks, man —

No problem, Carlos replied. Anytime.

The next morning, to make sure Thom didn't get too much of a taste of his own liberty, O'Brien made him go on commserv right away. His first day on the job, Thom joined Jeremy and Carlos outside the back of the Ryder, where Winston was waiting for them with a beat-up white pickup truck.

Sitting on the tailgate was an unsmiling, tall, tanned, muscular guy in his early twenties with a shaved head and wearing a black hoodie, jeans, and paint-covered coveralls. He wore enormous black wraparound shades that covered his eyes. Behind him, in the back of the pickup truck, Thom could see various brooms and brushes and rollers and cans of grey paint.

Good morning, gentlemen, Winston said. I hope you slept well last night because today you're going to crew together with Driscoll, who's going to lead you through a special kind of clean-up. And tomorrow. And the day after that. And the day after that.

Winston paused for effect.

Hopefully, Winston continued, after you've done a couple of hours of this work, you'll begin to understand that graffiti isn't art as so many of you claim, but an ugly form of vandalism that is a violation of public property — punishable by law, as you all know.

He looked at all of them with a hardened and unsympathetic pity.

Any questions? Winston asked, not waiting for a response. Good. Driscoll will take it from here.

Thom watched as Winston turned around and spoke quietly to Driscoll, obviously giving him instructions as he handed him a clipboard.

Still unsmiling, Driscoll stood up and looked at Thom and Jeremy and Carlos and nodded to his right, indicating a pile of grey coveralls on the tailgate of the truck.

Suit up, Driscoll said.

Jeremy and Carlos stepped forward and each selected a pair of coveralls, slowly pulling them over their jeans and t-shirts. Thom watched Jeremy and Carlos tentatively adjust them on their bodies, adapting to their new uniform.

As Winston walked away in the distance, Driscoll stared at his crewmates with a combination of numb hatred and curious revelry. Noticing that Thom wasn't putting his coveralls on like the others, Driscoll grabbed the last pair off the end of the truck and threw them directly at him.

Just like the label says, Driscoll said to Thom, his voice full of contempt, one size fits all.

In the truck, Jeremy and Carlos sat in the back while Thom sat up in front with Driscoll. It was a hot, muggy afternoon and as the heat crept into Thom's coveralls — the sweat dripping down his back — he was thankful for the cold blast of air conditioning that bombed out at him from the front vents.

When they arrived at their destination — one park in the city's winding maze of many parks along the river — Driscoll pulled into a parking lot and turned off the truck, and then pulled out a clipboard from between the seats. He nonchalantly flipped through the pages of paper, an amused, bittersweet expression on his face. Thom and Jeremy and Carlos sat silently, awaiting Driscoll's instruction.

All right, ladies, he said. Which of you sorry asses has done this before?

Carlos and Jeremy reluctantly stuck up their hands.

Good, Driscoll. So you two know the drill. Driscoll looked at Thom. What about you?

Never, Thom replied.

Well, then, Driscoll said bitterly. It's your lucky day.

Like unknown soldiers in their grey coveralls, Driscoll led

them across the green grass of the park, each of them carrying their cans of paint and paint trays and paint brushes and rollers toward their first destination: an underpass that had been heavily bombed in the past three days.

As Thom approached the underpass, staring at the graffiti that surrounded him — the walls thick with tag upon tag of activity: sprayed, stencilled, freestyle, wildstyle, word upon word intermeshed and interlinked, clogged with variant symbols, letters, voices, and styles — he began to see that whoever had been there last had somehow blended all of it together, joining the collective tags in blue and black, with intersecting lines of yellow and orange, keeping the integrity of the original tags while incorporating it into one giant piece in block letters: *AURA*.

Wow, whispered Carlos breathlessly beside Thom, that is *dope*.

As Thom stared at Aura's tag he began to see how his own piece would look: the fat, high-handed strokes, the orange and yellow lettering, accented by black and silver. The sizzling spark of the charge atop the two *T*s; the *N* bridging them in the middle. Or maybe it should just be the stick of dynamite itself? Red and orange, accented by silver and gold. Something to make people look, Thom thought. Take notice. And ask: *Who is this guy?* He knew he would have to draw it out a few times before he could get the flow of the letters right in his mind, see how it was going to write out as he held the spray can in his hand.

Hey, said a voice sharply, unmistakably Driscoll's. Quit balling and get to work.

Thom looked back at Driscoll, who glared at him. Obviously neither O'Brien nor Winston had told Driscoll of his investigation. As he turned away, he caught Jeremy's eye. Without missing a beat, Jeremy silently mouthed the word *asshole* and then continued painting. Thom looked down nervously and smiled. Jeremy was all right.

Thom turned back around and faced the pool of grey at his feet in his tray again and rolled the roller in it until it was soaked with paint, dripping with the non-existence of colour. *Tonight*, he thought, *tonight*. It had been exactly three weeks since he'd been caught, since he'd held a can of spray paint in his hand. He could hardly wait.

X.

Queen Mab called me today. At home. First thing this morning. Highly unusual. I drag myself to the phone, semi-comatose from working late again at the Ridgeway (and, dare I say, dancing with The DC at the Bridge), and she says to me all heavy and out of breath like she's been running a marathon: Have you seen it? Have you seen it yet?

And I say, slobbering into the phone, still half-asleep: What are you talking about? Have I seen *what*? And she says: TNT. The excitement barely contained in her voice. You know, like the stick of dynamite?

The thing you have to understand about Queen Mab is that she is an only child. Her parents, or at least I think her father, anyway, lives half the year in Bahrain or somewhere like that, working for some evil petroleum corporation. Her mother is some high-profile commercial real estate agent and the chair of some museum. They have so much money they don't know what to do with it. So they have their daughter, Queen Mab: the teeniest, tiniest, sprightliest wisp o' a thing, a teenage girl who's still so small she has to buy her clothes in the children's section. Seriously. For a good chunk of her preteen life, her parents dragged her all around the world to test her for this disease and that disease to find out what's wrong with her, but they found nothing. There is nothing wrong with her: she's just tiny. That's all. The only problem now is that after having all those tests done to her, Queen Mab really thinks that maybe, possibly, there is something wrong with her. Which is ridiculous. And we've all told her she's being ridiculous. But she refuses to believe us and has become incredibly superstitious.

Hence the tarot cards. Her longstanding romantic obsession with Chef BS. And her current fascination with signs. Not to mention learning ancient languages and how to cast spells. Sharp as a whip or a tack or an eagle or an axe: Queen Mab's mind never fails to startle me with its razor-like precision. This is why she's part of the G7, of course. She takes care of all the details no one else would think of. And besides — who else do you know that could cast a spell to protect us from evil? That girl just doesn't miss a thing.

Unfortunately, the only thing she can't tell me is where The Ten are. Somehow, despite my best efforts, she's "psychically blocked" in this area, along with any other relevant information about Story or Chef BS. We've tried so many times — through the cards, Ouija, automatic writing — but the end result is always the same. Nothing. Once, I thought we had a real clue to finding the Kalpa Path, but it just led us to the address of a Buddhist temple. Right path, wrong destination.

So, anyway, Queen Mab says to me that morning, Remember what I said? When I read your cards? About some kind of fire? An explosion, maybe? Yes, yes, yes, I slur back, wiping the drool from the corner of my lips, thinking, *Did The DC and I make out last night?* And then as Queen Mab's going on about dynamite being the pre-eminent symbol for fire, and *the* symbol for an explosion, as a signifier of what she had predicted actually coming true, I think to myself: why, yes, yes indeed, I *did* kiss The DC last night. No doubt about it. Long and hard, I believe. Did Chef see, I think to myself in a heart-thumping, pulse-jumping, blind-as-a-bat panic. Then I remember: the park, the trees, the wet grass. No, I believe not.

And then Queen Mab says impatiently (and very sweetly), in her delightfully singsongy voice, Are you listening to me? And I sigh a big huge sigh of relief and say to her, Yes, yes, I am. And then she says, No, you're not. And then she hangs up. Arrrrgh. So I wipe The DC from my mind like one of those dry-erase boards and I try to call her back but it's busy, and meanwhile my Mom is yelling at me through my bedroom door, asking, Do you want a ride this morning or not? I've got a meeting at nine, and I yell back, No thanks, Mom, I'll ride my bike, and then she says, Okay, bye, honey, have a nice day, and I say, You too, love you, and there's a distinct pause and then she finally says, Love you, too. And then she's gone, leaving me all alone to do what I want.

Which all goes to prove the No. 1 Most Important Thing I've learned about being part of the G7: to help my parents believe that I am still a good girl. Because being part of an elite underground counter-culture activist gang and street art crew isn't easy. Honestly. And the less suspicion I cause, the better. That's why I have a job. Why I do well in school. Why they would never dream that I do what I do, that I am who I am. Which is just the way I want it.

I get on my bike to go to the Ridgeway, and as soon as I'm outside I see the Graffpol must have been out yesterday in full force. They've been at it again. Erasing us out of the history that rightfully belongs to us. The future that we own. Big Brother, Chef calls him. Big Brother and the Graffpol. As I'm biking past, I can't help but feel sick at every grey wall I see, like a part of me is being erased. Devastated. Desolated. Desecrated. As if all the good work we did didn't even happen, or that the message the G7 is trying to spread doesn't really matter. We try so hard. And they just want to take it all away. Censor us from what we feel we need to say. Are our ideas so dangerous? Or are we just so forgettable that we can be silenced so easily? I guess that's why all the writers call this place Buff City.

Sometimes I wonder if that's the reason Story tried to catch out — she'd just had enough of the whole scene. She got tired of being buffed again and again. Her voice drowned out.

As I sped by on my bike, I saw the place where all my lovely writing had been buffed. Even though it was only ever meant to be temporary, I'll never get used to seeing it go away like that: disappearing into the landscape. And now there's nothing there but flat mucky clay grey walls.

And then, as I'm gliding hap-hap-happily along, I see it. What Queen Mab was talking about. TNT. A simple stick of dynamite with a single fuse, long and lean and tubular, with the flare of a stunning, multi-pointed star. In hot red and lovely orange, with sparkling silver and gold. Like, everywhere. Each one perfectly executed. Calmly. Without fear or trepidation. As if they didn't care whether they were going to get caught or not. Talk about hot.

Happily, Mr. Dy-no-mite did a tag right by where my piece had been: a lovely homage, all in glimmering gold. Hot hot hot. And very sexy. Threatening to ignite the city in a colossal and ecstatic orgiastic kaboom. Well. Va-va-voom.

Maybe Queen Mab was right. Maybe it is a sign.

XI.

The following morning, Thom woke up early after writing all night, unable to sleep. The city that he didn't know, that he had been made to discover, had opened itself up to him, offering all its walls and alleys, its secret spaces and hidden pathways for him to claim as his own, to make his mark. When he returned to the Ryder, he lay in his single bed in the darkness, listening to his heartbeat. His arm tugging with good, slow pain. Even though he'd worn gloves and a mask, he could still smell the spray in his hair, on his hands. Like an invisible skin, covering him. His whole body was charged with adrenalin, spiked with a happy fever that made him feel like he would never sleep again.

If he closed his eyes, he could remember everything. The arc of his hours fanning out in a chronology of who he had seen, where he had been. The closest he had come to being caught was early in the morning, in a park, by a couple staggering drunkenly together on the same path he was on. Not that he cared. They were too far away and too engrossed in each other to see him, but it had still unsettled him. Thom had watched with a curious jealousy as they collapsed into each other's arms in the grass, giggling and laughing.

But now he needed coffee. As he made his way into the kitchen, there was a young man sitting at one of the tables. Thom hadn't seen him before, and they eyed each other with an easy, cool suspicion. At the counter, Thom turned to the coffee maker. He needed to fuel up with caffeine if he was going to pull another slavish afternoon with Driscoll and then go out again that night.

Hey, you making coffee? the stranger said.

Yeah, Thom said, not turning around.

That's good, because I sure could use it. I still can't get used to the beds they got here, you know?

Yeah, Thom replied, as he reached for the coffee from the large tin on the counter and opened the resealable lid. I know.

I'm Omar, he said. I didn't meet you the other day 'cuz I was outta town, you know? At a court hearing.

Oh, Thom said. I'm —

Yeah, I know who you are. Carlos told me.

Thom turned around and looked at Omar. He was sitting casually in the chair, his hands resting behind his head. He smiled. Thom pretended to act indifferently to knowing that they had been talking about him, but it made the skin on the back of his neck crawl.

Heard you went out with the Graffpol yesterday, Omar said. Welcome to Buff fuckin' City, man.

Yeah, Thom said, unable to stop himself from smiling as he turned back to the coffee maker and carefully measured the grinds into the basket. Driscoll's a real piece of work.

Omar laughed quietly. He's not so bad, once you get used to him. He's actually got some cool stories to tell. Once he knows he can trust you.

Thom leaned over the sink and turned on the tap, watching the carafe fill up with water. Then he poured the water into the coffee maker and flipped on the power switch at the bottom.

What do you mean? Thom asked innocently, turning around again.

The smile was gone from Omar's face. This time he studied Thom intently with his dark brown eyes.

Heard you did a B & E. Where did you say you were from again? Omar asked.

Thom listened to the chug of the coffee maker, and then stared at Omar.

Oh, you know, here and there, he replied. I've been wandering for a while. Riding the rails, you know? The cops picked me up in the yards here. Tagging some trains and trespassing and all that.

A hopper, eh? continued Omar. That's some life. Dangerous, though. I couldn't do it. I'm too scared of that shit.

Thom looked down and laughed quietly.

Yeah, it's not for everyone.

As the coffee maker finished percolating, Thom poured himself and Omar a cup and sat down with him at the table. They sat across from each other in a strange but comfortable silence.

The smile returned to Omar's face. Obviously O'Brien's bogus story had passed the believability test.

Omar told Thom that Driscoll had been working as Winston's crew leader for a couple of years. Before that, Driscoll had been at the Ryder himself, after being caught tagging on a government building in broad daylight.

According to Omar, in his days as a writer, Driscoll was notorious for his throw-ups and burners, and could be seen everywhere, up all over the city. He was known for being the one willing to go to the heavens. Rooftops, fire escapes, abandoned buildings. He would eagerly scramble any structure, climbing to the top of anything he thought could be climbed. The city had seemed to him like a mountain range, each tag like a peak he had touched and stood out from, looking over the city below. Appropriately, the tag attributed to him was Everest, which was just a simple black triangle with an *E* at the top.

Then something happened. No one really knows what. The rumour, Omar said, was that Driscoll gave himself up: that he deliberately tried to throw up a burner on the wall of the government building in broad daylight because he *wanted* to get caught. He had had enough and so he sacrificed himself — not just to take down other writers, but to paint over all his pieces, to quash the scene. It was a whole new kind of style war. And it worked for a while, at first. But then, no matter how hard he tried, Driscoll couldn't keep up.

And then what happened? Thom asked, fascinated.

He gave up, Omar said, finishing his coffee. And Winston

recruited him. To make an example of his rehabilitation. C'mon
— think about it. You've seen all this motivational mountain
shit around, right? Winston gets to put *Everest* in his juvie.
To prove to the rest of the scene what the Ryder could do. Not
that it mattered, anyway. By that time the G7 were burning
everywhere.

The G7?

Omar grinned. Word. Chef BS and his crew doing all they do.

XII.

Just returned from a mind-bending flash mob. I was wondering when Chef was going to make the call. As soon as I got
the message this morning, the timing made perfect sense:
after 5:00 p.m. on a Friday, when everyone is racing home from
work, trying to pick up their last-minute items before they
head home, buying their cartloads of poisonous indulgences
for the weekend.

After being at the Ridgeway all afternoon, I got there as fast
as I could and took my place anonymously among the small
army of handpicked recruits that Chef had privately comman-
deered. Like them, I wandered the aisles of the store alone
with my empty shopping basket, among the frantic masses of
shoppers, ignoring Kane, The DC, Queen Mab, MC Lee, DJ
O'dysseus, and Chef as they ignored me, pretending to look at
industrial-sized packages of paper towel, cereal boxes, aerosol
spray, and blocks of cheese. Then, we all waited until 5:28 p.m.

There's something remarkable about a flash mob — time
stands still. I think that is truly its power. And everyone everywhere is so busy working, rushing here and there in their cars,
to and from houses and jobs and schools, to coffee shops and
malls and parking lots, that no one has any time. For anything.

It's their biggest complaint: I have no time. They are ruled by the fact that they have no time while they are being enslaved by the prospect of having more time.

In a flash mob we get to steal time back. Freeze it in its present form and bring attention to the moment of history that we're in, making others stop and consider their part in being a witness to that same moment.

I stood by the checkout, posing with my empty shopping basket. Promoting the most radical idea out there: buy nothing. Who says non-violent protest can't be powerful?

We held our individual poses for two minutes. Then resumed our anonymity among the other shoppers and gradually made our way out. Of all the people's reactions, the one I remember most was a little girl who was watching me with the most curious, beguiled expression. She could see that we were different from all the others, but the same, and that she was, too. When our time was up, she looked at me and smiled knowingly, like she had been given an answer to a big secret: that extraordinary things do happen.

Tonight we're going to celebrate. At the Bridge, of course. Chef's safe haven. Our refuge. The only place we will go. Besides, any place else just isn't the same. We have friends there, Chef BS says, saying nothing more. Then again, it doesn't hurt that Kane works the door. Or that DJ O'dysseus spins the wax. Or that the Library at the End of the Universe is above the dance floor.

But I will have to be careful tonight. Keep The DC's delicious little hands off of me. What fun that will be. Oh no, no, no, *mon chéri*, I will say to him. Not in front of ze Chef. We can rendezvous *après la danse*. Secretly. As we have been.

And now: to get ready. And I know just what I am going to wear: this stunning sapphire blue vintage dress I picked up at a thrift store for eight bucks. Flat shoes. And spike my silver hair high. Dance, dance, dance ... Talk about TNT: I'm the one who's going to sizzle tonight.

O, beautiful, beautiful life!

XIII.

When it was time to crew again with Driscoll, Thom was already at the back of the Ryder, waiting for him to arrive. Earlier that morning, Thom had asked Winston in private if he could work alone with Driscoll in the hopes of gaining more information on the G7. He eventually said yes, but at first Winston seemed skeptical, saying that "wasn't in the deal" he'd cut with O'Brien. Thom wondered exactly what kind of deal the two had made. For as soon as Thom mentioned calling O'Brien, Winston nervously backtracked his remarks, saying that it would "probably be fine" and that he would make the "necessary arrangements."

Thom heard Driscoll's truck before he saw it: rounding the curb with a dull roar and pulsating with a bluesy, thunderous beat. In the driver's seat, behind the immense warp of windshield, sat Driscoll. When he saw Thom, he pulled up beside him and rolled down the window.

Where's Carlos and Jeremy? Driscoll said above the deafening music.

Dunno. Thom shrugged.

Driscoll scoffed and pulled out his clipboard, following his finger down the page. Fucking Winston, Driscoll said as he threw the clipboard aside. Get in, he ordered. There's been a change. Just you and me from now on.

Thom played it cool and walked around to the passenger door and hopped in the truck. As they pulled out of the parking lot, Driscoll shot Thom a sideways glance and turned up the music even louder.

They drove, the stereo blasting, out of downtown and into the outlying streets of the city centre: down pretty, tree-lined avenues with manicured lawns and paved driveways, past stately heritage homes and estates lined with ambling briers of white roses, until they descended a steep hill and arrived at another park. It was the same park Thom had seen when he had first arrived: wide and green and edged along the river, with a giant concrete embankment. He had thought he might find it when he'd been out the night before, but he hadn't made it this far.

Thom sat awash in the wave of sound in the cab of the truck, feeling the afternoon sun bear down on him. He felt so tired. Just the thought of working all afternoon with Driscoll exhausted him. He would have to sleep before he went out again tonight or else he wouldn't make it through tomorrow. Or the day after that. Thom began to realize that he had been snagged into the cruel circle of O'Brien's punishment. Sure, he could write all night. But only if he could work all day. O'Brien eventually knew one or the other would catch up with him, and he couldn't get out of working with Driscoll.

Here we are, Driscoll said, turning off the engine and staring out the windshield. Graffiti fucking alley. This is where they all come — to put their signature out in the world, to put their mark on the wall. Straight from the 'burbs with a can of spray paint they stole out of their parents' garage. Latchkey kids with nowhere to go and nothing to do from the time they finish school to the time their parents come home who think they got something to say about the world.

After what Omar had told him, Thom couldn't believe how embittered Driscoll had become. Though as he followed Driscoll's gaze to a wall under a bridge, he saw it was covered with small, uninspired tags, scratched out in permanent black marker, wax crayon, and spray paint. Amongst them were some stickers and posters, plastered randomly on the wall.

Fucking toys, Driscoll scorned. Amateurs.

Following Driscoll's lead, Thom opened the door and walked to the back of the truck, where they suited up in their coveralls and grabbed their painting supplies.

As they walked toward the wall, Driscoll went on with his lament, filling the void of silence between them.

I mean, what's with these kids? They keep tagging and we keep painting over it, hoping one day they're gonna get the fucking message, but they don't. They just keep doing it. Who do they really think they are? Do they really think anyone gives a rat's ass about them?

Driscoll stopped and turned to face Thom and pushed his sunglasses up onto his forehead. His eyes were a remarkable deep sea green. He stared straight at Thom.

I knew people who were writers, he confessed. Like you. But they never did shit like this. They were kings, you know? Now I'm just *weary* of looking at these toys. Tags, bombs, dress-ups thrown up, everywhere, all these kids trying to get all *city status*. Everywhere I go I'm reminded of their ambition, their ignorance, their mediocrity. Sometimes I wish all the graff in this entire fucking city could be just wiped clean. All of it. Erased. This isn't graffiti, this isn't art, this is just *pollution*. It interrupts my vision; it denies me from seeing what I want to see. I'm happy to buff it. There's nothing more I'd rather do.

Thom stared back at Driscoll, knowing that this would be the best time to ask him about his work as a writer, about the G7 — something, anything — but Thom felt too intimidated by him to say anything: if anyone was going to be the first to find out he was a rat, it was Driscoll.

The rest of the afternoon, Driscoll and Thom worked side by side together in silence, painting over the wall. It was the hardest work he had done yet, and before his shift was over he had to climb up the side of the wall to reach the ledge of an overhang where there was even more graffiti. Thom teetered on the edge of the rusted steel platform, directing his roller over the poured concrete, covering up the spray paint. He recognized some of the same names he had seen elsewhere: Ruse, Snare, Down, Pile. These were more accomplished than the other tags on the wall — harder to reach, more exposed, risky — but Thom could tell Driscoll was unimpressed.

As he worked, Driscoll's angry words echoed inside Thom's head. Sure, some of the tags were crap. But the kids had to start somewhere. Didn't they? They weren't going to get any better sitting in their bedrooms, doodling on their homework. Graffiti, as Thom understood it, was a total sensory experience — something that needed to be experienced outdoors. It shouldn't matter if it gets painted over, or ripped down, or torn away. Surely Driscoll would have understood that, out of anybody. The temporary nature of the work itself — now you see it; now you don't— was what made it powerful.

While Thom finished buffing the wall, he took a moment to look around. He saw the park and the embankment and how the river forked away in two different directions, leading into the northern and southern parts of the city. Then, in the distance, above, he saw a train bridge that he hadn't seen before, and on its rust-red side was a stencil of a tiger, spray-painted white. It seemed to be semi-floating in mid-air, roaring in a position of attack over a seat of multicoloured flames.

Hey, do you see that? Thom called to Driscoll, pointing toward it.

He was surprised to feel his heart pounding. Not with fear,

but with excitement. The stencil was magnificent: the best piece Thom had seen yet. Over the tiger's head was a crown.

Driscoll stopped painting and looked at Thom and followed the direction of his arm.

Tyger Tyger burning bright, in the forests of the night: what immortal hand or eye, dare frame thy fearful symmetry? Driscoll said.

Thom was confused. What?

William Blake, Driscoll said flatly. Don't you read poetry?

Thom shook his head, still confused. No.

Well, you should, Driscoll replied, turning back to painting the wall. Especially if you *ever* want to get laid again. Besides, poetry is the key to opening the cage of the soul.

Thom stared at Driscoll in disbelief. Who said that?

Driscoll stared back at him. I did. Now get back to work. We're not going after any tigers today. That's too dangerous a climb for you.

As they were driving back through downtown to the Ryder, Thom saw a place called the Bridgewater Tavern.

From the sidewalk, it looked like a seedy, dishevelled building with cracked and peeling paint; its high, arched Victorian windows blacked out with silver reflective backing. Above the main entrance was an old neon sign that hung from the building over the street: *The Bridgewater Tavern, est. 1903.*

That, said Driscoll matter-of-factly, noticing where Thom was looking, is the Bridge. The only place to really go in town. If you don't have a curfew.

Do you go there? Thom asked Driscoll.

He looked at Thom with a mix of scorn and disdain and barked with black laughter. What? Me? No way.

Thom looked at the empty buildings on the other side of

the street. The *For Lease* signs were too many to count. Driscoll leaned forward and cranked up the stereo. Thom had hoped Driscoll might say more, but it was clear he had finished talking for the day. Ever since he had seen the tiger stencil, he had seemed distant and preoccupied, lost in his own thoughts.

The brilliance of the tiger stencil, Thom figured out, was not just in its location, but in how the white paint had been used over the red to actually burn the image of the tiger onto the retina of the viewer. So what was on the wall became a burning white tiger in the air, the residual flash of the afterimage still burning in the viewer's mind. If Driscoll knew who had done the tiger — which Thom suspected he did — he wasn't saying.

That night, Thom covered as much territory as he could. Scattering tags helter-skelter here and there along the bike path and on garbage pails, mailboxes, posts, stop signs. Bombing over walls he had painted with Driscoll only a few hours ago. He was curious to see what Driscoll's reaction to his work would be. What remark he might make.

But he knew in order to compete with the other writers in the city — to really get up — he had to make a burner. And it had to be dope. So he went to the embankment, and it was there, under the bright lights of the adjacent baseball field, on a blank canvas of concrete, that Thom put up the first of his giant scale TNT burners on the high, lit wall.

Thom made the letters look as if they were in a suspended state of explosion: bursting with the possibility of destruction. When the piece was finished, he went across the bridge to admire his work from the other side. When he reached the top of the adjacent steep hill, he sat on a high grassy slope and stared across the darkness over the river, admiring its size and scope, the way the letters appeared to be lit from within, their explosion imminent.

On his way back to the Ryder, Thom went downtown, hoping to find other pieces. He was curious to seek out more of the tiger stencils, but also to find more of the G7's work, to see if there was a pattern to where they wrote. Or how. But as he wandered the back alleyways, he was disappointed with what he found. All of it seemed uninspired, except for one piece: a flock of birds, in black, flying out from the pages of an open book, the words *Story, RIP* written underneath.

As he wound his way through the downtown city streets, Thom saw the bar that Driscoll had shown him earlier: the Bridge. Outside the main door, a long lineup filled the sidewalk. As he walked past, Thom could hear the hypnotic pulse of music from upstairs. Knowing he'd never get in through the lineup, Thom looked at the buildings surrounding it, strategizing how he could get up the back fire escape of the building and onto the upper roof patio. Just because Driscoll wouldn't let him climb earlier that day didn't mean that he couldn't do it.

Twenty minutes later, Thom was standing on the floor in front of the DJ, dancing with the crowd, aglow in the radiant white light. It had been so long since he had been out. He couldn't even remember the last time he had danced. But tonight he was a stranger — even to himself — and since no one knew who he was, he didn't even know or care if someone was watching him.

Thom just closed his eyes and lost himself in the music, letting himself go.

XIV.

Somehow I knew when I left the house tonight that something was going to happen.

I don't know why I felt that way. It could have had something to do with the E I took, but as soon as I stepped out of my parents' house into the soft, warm night and walked down the street I felt like I was swimming through air. Like there was a kind of magic everywhere. Because the sun was setting and everything was glowing orange like it was slowly burning and I just closed my eyes and made a kind of wish that I would be able to find The Ten.

Before going down to the Bridge, I walked around downtown, looking down my favourite alleyways, thinking that I'd find a clue waiting there for me. And then when I didn't find one, I'd throw up my own little tag with my Sharpie and wander down the next one, and then the next one after that, looking to see if she would appear, in a magic kind of way, like she does in my dream.

And then I don't know what happened or why. I can't explain it. But I could almost feel for certain that she had been where I had been, that our footsteps had crossed each other's in the same street and that the air that I breathed was the same that she had breathed in, too. And as I drank in the sweet, sultry air it was like I was drinking her in, my lips tingling as if we had kissed. Finally, in a daze, like she was telling me where to go, I followed her scent like it was an invisible line around this corner, and then the next, until it led me to the Bridge, where I knew The DC and the rest of the G7 would be. And as I floated up the stairs, all my thoughts of her disappeared when I saw the blinding hot white lights of the Bridge.

And then it was bang smash all music big: the universe in a supernova of cosmic flash and debris and me pushing through the wall of yielding bodies that felt like a wave of ocean surf and I felt a hand reach out for me. I saw The DC's sweet, smiling face looking at me through the tube of the wave, his diamond ear studs twinkling like two hot stars, and my heart got all big in my throat as I thought about how he had kissed me the other night, and he shouted at me above the music something I couldn't hear but I nodded and laughed and smiled anyway, and then he was thrusting something cold in my hand and I took it and drank it down fast.

Then The DC led me across the dance floor and into the blue corner where we always sit, where Chef and Queen Mab and MC Lee were already there waiting. Kane out on the floor and DJ O'd in the booth. MC Lee looked fabulous in a vintage silver lamé dress accented only by one giant rhinestone cocktail ring glowing like a cluster galaxy on her forefinger. Her dark, almond-shaped eyes as big as moons as she watched The DC get me more to drink, his arm brushing suggestively against mine. MC Lee looked at me and smiled.

Everything I know about MC Lee is what she told me herself. Her parents were immigrants who opened a convenience store. From the moment she came to this country, she was expected to take every opportunity that came to her. To take her rightful place in society. To be better; do more. She couldn't help it. She had to fulfill her parents' expectations. To exceed them.

But guess what? Nudge nudge wink wink — I learned from The DC that Kane and MC Lee had a fling once. So I do have something on her, if I need it — besides her sympathy. Chef's Rule is (and I quote): "Do not date, mate, or fornicate with any fellow member of our tribe." We know, thanks to Mab, that the only reason he imposed it was to protect us from what had happened between him and Story.

Anyway. My brain is still buzzing and I'm sitting there with MC Lee and Queen Mab and we're listening to the genius beats sweet DJ O'd is laying down and for a moment it's like my world is a beautiful white sheet and I can pick it up by the four corners and wrap myself in it and wave it in the wind. Go out to sea. Fly up to the stars. Like I can gather up everything I own and carry it in my own two hands. I let this image play in my mind: the breeze of the white sheet fanning the arc of my thoughts. Around me everyone is dancing, happy, and the energy of everyone and everything around me is like a giant pulse I can feel thumping in the vein of the universe.

And then I see him.

Wearing black jeans and a white t-shirt. A beautiful boy. Like a single flame of light burning in the sea of other bodies, as if he had stepped through from a dream, come from another place and time.

I can't help but stare at him, taking him in: the lean signature of his bones as he bends into the light, dancing angelic, possessed, with a kind of ecstatic frenzy, but in slow motion, as if being kicked from within, on the downbeat reaching up and stealing a piece of air like it was his last breath and releasing it like there was a little white bird hidden in the palm of his hand. His eyes closed.

I can't move. My whole body goes into full flower: instantly in bloom. And I just stand there, watching him, electric with wonder. Want. Desire like little sparks shooting off from my heart, a bomb ticking in the centre of my skin.

And I'm staring at him —and then somehow he sees *me*, and he looks at me and suddenly it's like all the music stopped and everyone stopped dancing and it was just me and him and my heart kinda went boom. The voltage travelling all the way through my body, right down to my fingertips. Like lightning in a long slow burn.

And we're having this moment. This intense psychic moment. And then boom again, my heart is over the initial blast and my head is singing, and The DC is thrusting another cold drink in my hand and telling me Chef wants to talk to me. He shoots me a wild-eyed stare, naked with jealousy, wondering exactly who the f-u-c-k is the guy I am so obviously entranced with.

I go and sit beside Chef, and as soon as I do, he throws his arm around me and whispers in my ear how beautiful I look and how proud he is of me and the work I've done for the G7. The smell of his body drifts up around me, vaguely sweet and musky, like an animal. I sit awash in his praise for a star-studded moment as his silvery voice sings in my ear. I gush, taking all of him in while I surreptitiously scan the dance floor, searching for the beautiful boy. Tragically, he is gone. Vanished. Out of sight. The DC stares at me with Chef. I try to appear calm, relaxed. Happy. Nod. But inside, all I can think about is where the boy has gone.

After Chef releases me, I move out onto the dance floor and am swallowed into the hot womb of darkness, bodies surrounding me. I allow myself to be pulled into the crowd and get lost in the crush of skin and sweat, riding on waves of joy. And then I close my eyes. Make a wish. And when I open them, there he is, dancing right there in front of me. His eyes still closed, like he's dreaming.

I stare at him in my oh-so-E-nlightened state. Slightly staggering in front of him. As if I am on the ledge of a high mountain. Spindrift clouds in my hair. Not even daring to take one step closer for fear that I might fall. But, oh, the view. And I just stand there, my eyes wide open, looking at him like that, everyone moving around us.

Then he opens his eyes and looks at me and smiles. Neither scared nor surprised. As if he knew I would be there. As if there was no other place I would rather be.

Then I feel someone's hand on my lower back. I turn and look. It's MC. Of course. This being our little game we like to play. So we dance. The two of us, together. Wordlessly moving, our eyes closed. High enough not to care that somewhere I know both Chef and The DC are watching.

But when I open my eyes again, he's gone. Just like that. And just MC Lee is standing in front of me, swivelling her hips and outstretching her arms like some glittering supernova in the night. I look left; right. The beautiful boy is nowhere to be seen. And then, out of the corner of my eye, I see him walking off the dance floor, down the hallway, and out onto the upper roof patio. I follow him, watching as he slips, unnoticed, over the edge of the rooftop patio and along the edge of the building to a fire escape that leads down to the alley.

And it strikes me in a vision, as I watch him get swallowed up into the darkness of the city, that Story sent him to me. That tonight, she, from the realm of my dreams, delivered me a messenger to help me find her, to find The Ten.

XV.

Thom opened his eyes, not knowing where he was.

Then, as he took in the surroundings — the white tile floor and the small, narrow bed he found himself sleeping in — he slowly began to realize where he was: in his own room, at the Ryder.

From the first time he had left his parents' house, he had been constantly on the move, staying in place to place for short periods of time, moving on when he needed to, not knowing where he would stay next. As a result, he often woke up, panicked, not knowing where he was. He was disoriented because the world around him hadn't had a chance to imprint itself upon his body. He'd read about it once. It was called nomadic memory.

Thom rolled over and got up, dragging himself toward the window, and pulled back the stiff, grey, sun-stained curtains. It was early morning. The sun blazed on the river, diamond glitter.

It was so bright it hurt Thom's eyes to look at it. But he couldn't look away. He felt mesmerized by it, seduced by its beauty. Like them. The people he'd seen at the Bridge last night. The guy in the white suit with the eye patch. The girl. Thom couldn't stop thinking about them. Or her. Who was she?

As he stared out over the river, Thom heard a knock at his door. He hoped maybe it was Carlos or Omar. He had so much he wanted to ask them.

It's open, he said.

Morning, a voice said calmly.

Thom looked back to see Winston enter Thom's room and close the door behind him.

Oh, Thom said, trying to hide the disappointment in his voice. Hey.

It struck Thom that even though Winston knew all the details of Thom's case, the two of them still hadn't really sat down and talked or gotten to know each other. Thom studied Winston's loose-fitting clothes, his ragged grey ponytail. There was something about Winston he couldn't quite explain: a feeling, an intuition, perhaps. Thom wasn't sure what it was. Only that it was there.

Winston sat down in a chair. So. How are things going?

Thom shrugged. Good, I guess.

And how's it going with Driscoll? Winston continued, inquisitively. Everything working out okay?

Thom wasn't sure if this was the point in the conversation where he and Winston could stop pretending and just talk freely. He wasn't even sure what kind of information Winston was expecting him to provide. Or when. But since Winston hadn't asked Thom for the answer to a specific question, he assumed that this would be how they would talk: in a doublespeak of cryptic exchange.

Sure, fine, Thom said. No problems.

After a moment of uncomfortable silence, Winston flashed him a small, patronizing smile.

Good, good.

It was clear that this conversation was as painful to him as it was to Thom. But he wasn't giving anything away.

Thom turned and looked out the window again, staring at an old abandoned couch that was sitting in the middle of the river on a section of dry riverbed. Behind it, a fountain fanned out in a trio of shooting arcs of water and mist, into the forked basin of the river.

Thom thought of the spray paint and paint markers under his bed. He was running low. I need more *supplies*, Thom said, turning back to Winston. I'm almost out.

Winston nodded matter-of-factly, though Thom was pretty sure he could see Winston wincing at the thought of sneaking some cans o' Rusto through the back door of the Ryder.

When do I report to you? Thom asked, half turning his head.

You don't, Winston answered flatly. Everything goes to O'Brien. He'll contact you. When he needs to. Or if you need to.

But what will you do? Thom asked.

I will provide you with your most basic necessities. I will protect your identity. But I will neither help nor hinder you.

What was it about Winston? Thom thought to himself. Despite his easygoing way with the other guys at the Ryder, he was stern and quiet. Thom recalled the quiet drive they'd shared in the car his first day: O'Brien sitting stonily in the front while Winston drove, gloomily staring ahead into the traffic.

And I will answer any questions, if you have them, Winston concluded. Anything else?

No, Thom said as he leaned against the windowsill. He heard Winston turn around and move toward the door. No, wait. Yes,

I have a question. He turned around and faced Winston. Who are the G7?

You mean you didn't do your homework before you came here? Winston remarked. I thought O'Brien would have told you everything.

Thom could have sworn he saw a smirk on Winston's face. He didn't have the balls to tell him that O'Brien had already told him everything he knew. Which pretty much amounted to Sweet FA. Whoever they were, the G7 had done a sweet job of hiding their identities from the public. And staying clear of the law.

Were any of them ever *held* here? The word stuck like a barb in Thom's throat.

Winston stared curiously at Thom, unblinking, as if he had misheard the question. The G7? he repeated. He slowly bowed his head. Uh, no, he replied.

Wow, Thom said in disbelief. It's like they're untouchable or something.

Something like that, Winston said quietly.

Thom instantly realized why Winston disliked him so much: his very presence threatened the Ryder's viability and existence as a rehabilitation centre, not to mention Winston's role in managing it. If Winston couldn't nab the G7 and turn a bunch of writers into born-again citizens of the world, then what good was he? Or the Ryder?

Thom studied Winston's face, knowing that he knew what he knew, or at least suspected.

I'll get you those things in the next few days, Winston said, changing the subject.

Sure, Thom answered. Thanks.

Then Winston quietly left the room, closing the door behind him. Soon it would be time for Thom to open the door and keep it open all day — the Ryder's version of an open door policy that allowed for complete transparency between all of its inhabitants. There were no secrets because there was nothing to hide; everything was visible.

That was another reason why Winston disliked him: Thom's covert operation and code of secrecy undermined Winston's whole philosophy. But Thom couldn't worry about that now. He really did have a job to do. And he was going to do it. The first place he knew he would have to go was back to the Bridge. To find him. And her. Everything started with them.

XVI.

My delirium continues after yesterday. What more can I say? My whole soul just melts into whisky, drunk with just the slightest thought. Of him. And me. Of what sweet lovely honey we will be. Sipping kisses in the elixir dream light. Whatever date fate chooses, I can hardly wait to see him again. At the Bridge or anywhere. And next time I won't be afraid. To say hi. To dance with him. To do anything. Because how can that be a bad thing? It's not against the rules to date someone outside the G7.

The DC, however, as it turns out, is rather jealous for someone who is not supposed to be, and last night kept asking me who *he* was. Why, I said, should it even matter considering that me and The DC aren't even supposed to be together? Or had he forgotten The Rule? The Rule that we had been very good at breaking?

Then The DC accused me of being callous because he thought we really had something, and then he leaned over to kiss me, and because I couldn't stop thinking of the beautiful boy at the Bridge and how he might kiss me, I let him, and then I had to pull away and tell The DC to stop. It was all so clichéd.

I had to tell him we couldn't go on this way. We had to be true. To The Rule. For the cause, I said. To Chef. For the G7's sake. No matter what our feelings are. Or were.

Sadly, however, I don't think The DC feels the same way. Because then he accused me of being with Chef, which I said was totally ridiculous. And then he said he saw the way I was with him at the Bridge the other night and I said that was crazy because Chef was just telling me how much he loved my work and The DC said sure he was.

The DC and I fought all the way to Io. When we arrived there together, Chef was already waiting for us. Kane and DJ O'dysseus were there too, along with MC Lee and Queen Mab, wondering what took us so long. Of course The DC and I got a few knowing stares. But I don't care what the rest of them think. It's definitely over between us. Chef quickly took The DC aside as we all fit in the front room of the trailer, Kane sparking up a spliff, me and DJ O'dysseus taking a hit or two. MC Lee doesn't do dope, period. But when Chef took a big drag and put on this trippy record called *L'Apocalypse des animaux*, I watched while even Queen Mab took a toke. I couldn't believe it. Normally she doesn't smoke up but I guess there's a first time for everything.

Then Chef started telling this crazy tale about a boy who thought he was from outer space. The boy was like a star, Chef said: hard and bright and beautiful when seen from afar, but too hot and dangerous to be seen up close. He lived all alone in the far reaches of outer space, the blackness of the universe all around him.

Then one day something appeared. It was like nothing he had ever seen before. It was slow moving, a dull shining mark that crawled through the canopy of blackness. At first he believed it must have been a comet, since he had seen one of those long ago, and he thought that he recognized its same slow trawl, hurtling frozen across the sky. But it was not. It was a planet of some kind. He couldn't tell how big or how small.

He watched it from afar, studying its champagne sparkle, its erratic glow. Then he noticed that it could change colours, and switch from green to red, then blue and purple. Most remarkable of all was that the planet appeared to grow, and got bigger day by day, hour by hour. Then the boy realized that it wasn't getting bigger, but that it was moving through space, coming directly toward him.

How does one contemplate the demise of one's existence when one can clearly see it coming? Chef asked us. The boy realized quickly that there was nothing he could do. So he set about preparing for what would be the moment of his collision with this object from afar. As it came closer, it became obvious to him that it was a deep space object, and much larger than he could ever have imagined.

The closer it came he realized that the reason it changed colour was that it was spinning so violently, whirling uncontrollably within its own gravitational velocity. The colours, too, he realized were storms: swirling masses of gaseous clouds that swarmed over the surface of the planet. The champagne sparkle that he had seen earlier was nothing more than a clutter of asteroids: a halo of cosmic debris.

Still, the boy watched it hurtle, spinning wildly, toward him, his heart filled with a terrible kind of love, in awe of what he knew was eventually going to happen to him. Because he had never been touched by someone or anything so close before; no one had dared to come that near to him, for fear of getting burned or hurt, damaged in some degree, by him. So he waited. And waited.

Finally, after what seemed an eternity, the day came, Chef said, when the boy heard the sound. Which was something that he hadn't expected. Since you don't think of sound in space. But this planet that was coming toward him had a sound. It sang. In a voice that was both low and resonant, but sweet and light, like a whisper. It was like nothing he had ever heard before and he was seduced by it as the planet headed straight toward him.

As it approached, the turbulence was extraordinary, and the boy felt the storms and winds of the planet encircle him until at last he felt his starry burning body crash against the swirling mass of the planet, and in that moment, Chef said, there was a sound between them that quaked with sonic reverberations as their energies collided. Everything seemed to move in slow motion, in immeasurable gaps of time and space, bending and stretching all dimensions.

The boy had thought he would be destroyed instantly, but in fact something more extraordinary happened. Remarkably, the boy seemed to be absorbed by the other planet, as if he were liquid that had passed through its central core. And after he had passed through it, the planet stopped swirling wildly and the storms ceased, the asteroids drifted off into deep space, and the colours of the planet intensified to a deep radiant glow. And the sound! The sound of the planet was a sweet ambient hum, an intoxicating harmony of notes that spun out into a complex system of rings.

And the boy and the planet are still there, he said, in their special corner of the universe, entranced with each other, held captive in each other's energies. Together, they're making a sound that will never reach our ears, but, if we listen very carefully, we may still be able to hear the echo in the flap of a bird's wing or in the trickle of a mountain stream, since everything that is happening in outer space is connected to what is happening here on Earth. We are not separate from that, Chef said, pointing to the star-filled sky; we are that.

We are all made of stars, he said.

XVII.

Driscoll and Thom stood side by side in front of the large cement column under the train bridge, staring at the enormous burner in front of them. One could clearly read the letters *TNT*, in alternating lines of black and orange and silver.

Well, said Driscoll with contempt. Looks like we got a new king trying to *get up on the scene.* The sarcastic emphasis in Driscoll's voice daggered the air between them.

Thom stared hard at it, trying desperately not to betray his true feelings to Driscoll about the work. Especially now that he saw it in the sunlight. It was hard for him to believe that he had created it only a few hours ago.

This guy must have been at it all night long, Driscoll said angrily. Let's get to work.

Thom followed Driscoll to the back of the truck, where he loaded up his paint tray, refilling it with the familiar grey, putty-coloured paint he'd grown so accustomed to seeing. The smell was different from spray paint: earthy, somehow. Wet.

You start on this one, while I do the other one down there. Driscoll pointed down the path. And hurry up, because it looks like TNT went on a fucking bender. We may have to pull a double.

Thom sighed with disappointment. Driscoll was quick to notice Thom's reaction.

What's the matter? Got a date with your parole officer?

As Driscoll laughed, Thom grabbed his paint tray and roller and made his way toward the column. He placed the paint tray down on the ground in front of his feet and gripped the handle of the roller, dipping it in the paint and rolling it against the ridged section of the tray.

Then he thought of her.

The beautiful girl at the Bridge. He couldn't stop thinking of her.

Thom turned and faced the burner and began, systematically, painting over it, starting in the upper left-hand corner. Trying to ignore the feeling that he'd just been stabbed in the gut. Because here he was, buffing his own piece. Dull hate surged in him. For Driscoll, for Winston, for O'Brien. For all of them. Thom stared at the bleak, featureless wall in front of him. He felt like he was being slowly forced to die, like he had to kill off one of the most important parts of himself.

Aren't you done yet? he heard Driscoll shout at him.

Thom, finishing up, dreaded how many more of his own walls he would have to do, still hating the fact that he could do nothing except what Driscoll told him.

Driscoll watched Thom finish up with a smug satisfaction.

That looks better, said Driscoll. Now, let's keep going. We've got a lot of work to do. This shit is everywhere.

Thom didn't even realize the time until Driscoll told him they were done for the day. Exhausted, Thom stared at the grey paint on his hands, the incidental blisters. As he carried his equipment back to the truck, Driscoll came up behind him.

Good work today, he said.

Thom said nothing.

I know, Driscoll said to him blithely, you hate me. I don't blame you. I'd hate me if I were you, too.

Driscoll lifted his sunglasses and looked Thom in the eye.

Your problem is you're still too close to the graffiti to see it for what it truly is: vandalism. You see these tags and you think they're radical, an alternative voice of the people ... whatever. You may even call it art. But it's not. Believe me. Especially in this no-name town. No one has the guts to do something really extraordinary. Shit. They all sneak around at night, in back alleys and under train bridges, marking out their territory like they're living in some south L.A. slum, playing tough, acting out their little turf games. They know nothing. About life. Or art.

Thom stared at Driscoll. He wanted to say something to him but realized that there was nothing he could say. Thom made his way to the cab of the truck and sat down inside, waiting for Driscoll to drive him back to the Ryder. He watched him close the tailgate in his rear-view mirror, reading the words *Objects in mirror are closer than they appear.* Thom considered the irony of this, since he wasn't getting any closer to Driscoll.

After what seemed forever, Driscoll finally opened his door and hopped inside.

I know you think I'm an asshole, Driscoll shouted as he leaned forward and turned up Led Zeppelin on the stereo. But that's okay. We all need people to hate in this life, and I'm happy to be one of them. Call it a kind of duty.

Thom looked over at Driscoll. Thanks a lot, he said.

Driscoll laughed as he weaved in and out of traffic. No problem.

For the next few minutes they drove on through the downtown without talking. The music a wall between them. He looked out the window into the street. It was a beautiful, warm summer's evening, but the streets were void of people, the sidewalks filled with a kind of luxurious emptiness. A few people straggled out of restaurants or stood lingering in front of bars, but other than those few, there were no people anywhere. It was like a ghost town, Thom thought, but a ghost town from the future. A city where only the corporate zombies came out during the day and everyone else stayed inside, hidden away in their homes, sitting in front of their computers, their televisions, held hostage in a completely virtual world.

Thom watched the *For Lease* signs blur past. Finally, as they were approaching the main intersection of downtown, Thom saw a giant set of words in black capital letters spray-painted along the side of a vacant building: *Evolution is in Revolution.*

Thom stared at it in awe. Then he said to Driscoll, That's the G7, right?

Driscoll stared at it through the windshield and scoffed, looking away in disgust.

Who are they? Thom asked

Driscoll stared up ahead at the light, disinterested. A bunch of fucking losers, that's who, Driscoll said. He swung his arm up and pointed at it, violently jabbing the air with his middle finger. Do they *really* think anyone gives a shit about their clever, self-important, ironic, hipster, neo-Marxist ideologies? Driscoll's voice dripped with rage. It's fucking bullshit.

Thom watched a group of young teens throng at the corner. The light changed and Driscoll stepped on the gas. As they sped through the intersection, Thom noticed some of them casting an interested glance back at the wall, obviously reading the message.

Maybe Driscoll was right, Thom thought. But then again, maybe he wasn't.

When they got back to the Ryder, Thom gathered his gear and went to open his door only to find it was locked. He looked at Driscoll, who was grinning at him with an evil fuck-you stare.

You don't want to hold my hand and take me inside, do you? Thom shot at him.

Driscoll looked at him. After all the hand jobs you've given yourself? Not a fucking chance.

Open the fucking door, Thom said.

Driscoll smiled and unlocked the door. See, I knew you could use your big words.

You know what? Thom said as he opened the door and got out of the truck. You're right. You are an asshole.

Driscoll smiled and said nothing.

XVIII.

There are times when I feel like life is just a four-letter word. And then there are times when I feel like the magic forces that are at work in the universe are doing what they do just for me. It's just like what Mab had said would happen. When she said I would encounter some force: *some kind of flame. A fire. Some kind of explosion.*

I was biking back from the Ridgeway when I saw someone standing in the dark half-light along the long cement wall near the Oxford bridge, dressed in a hoodie and jeans slung low, the soles of their high-tops touching the floor of the earth. Not scanning left to right, nervous, watching. But calmly placed before the wall, in full view for all to see, holding a spray can in one hand. Not caring who saw. It's so rare in this city to see anyone so openly bomb a wall. What with the Graffpol and such. I was intrigued. So I got off my bike and watched.

At first I wondered if it was anyone we knew. The G7 knows most of the writers in town, either by name, reputation, or association. And Chef BS has had a long history here. Kane had been one of the most prolific taggers in the city before he was approached by Chef to join the G7. Just like me.

I stared at the figure again, studying it more closely. It was most definitely a he, not a she. I could tell by the shoulders. The hands. The way he stood back on one foot, looking at what he'd done. And then he began to spray a line in bright, metallic silver.

Big, fat, geometric letters. That he filled in with a bright, glossy black. It was brilliant. Made more so by his precision, his calm exactitude. His steady hand drawing clean, fluid lines. Watching him was completely mesmerizing: seeing how he flicked his wrist, twisting his arm, shaking the can, bending over, up, stretching down. How he would lean back and look. Shoulders back, relaxed. His head turning. This way, then that.

Finally he brought out a can of orange spray paint and added the last few details, the metallic hue shining like a thin stream of fire being shot out of the tip. I watched with awe and lust and fascination, wondering how he managed to stay so focused and relaxed. Not once did his body betray any fear or anxiety about being caught. It was like he knew it was never going to happen. Or maybe he just didn't care. I didn't know what was more alluring. My heart stopped. It was a *T*. Followed by an *N*. And another *T*.

And then he turned around.

TNT is *him*. The beautiful boy I saw at the Bridge.

Hey, I said to him when he had finished. You could get into trouble for that, you know.

He turned around and looked at me. Took me in with his eyes and smiled, grinning a mischievous smirk. You think? he said. I studied his lean, strong arms, watching him as he pushed back messy dark brown hair. His face was stubbly, and he looked slightly dishevelled, like he hadn't slept in a few days. In fact, he looked like he was wearing the same clothes I had seen him wear at the Bridge a few nights before. Then I met his sparkling light brown eyes. And my heart went boom. Again. And I smiled at him and said, yeah. Though it wouldn't be for being amateur. You seem to know what you're doing.

He smiled at me again and our eyes locked, and for a moment it seemed like he and I were the only two people in the world, and that world was a beautiful place. Everything came into focus: the

trees were greener and the river was cleaner and the air that blew
between us was soft and perfumy sweet and the wall behind him
burst into a kaleidoscope of colour and light and I kind of felt
like I was floating on a little fluffy cloud, wings fluttering under
my feet.

TNT, I said. That's some tag you got. You're blowing up the
city, you know that?

He laughed softly. Like the way nice guys do, all shy and
abashed. But cool, too.

Yeah, he replied. Guess so.

He looked me in the eye again. My heart stopped again.

Haven't I seen you before? he said to me as he stepped away
from the wall and walked toward me. Maybe, I replied, acting
coy. Where would it have been?

He stood in front of me. A big magnet pull between us.
Electricity city. Like I'm talking. Serious. Voltage. Like I'd never
ever felt with anybody ever before. And I mean that in the most
sincere and honest way. It's like he had a U magnet hidden
inside his hoodie and I was Iron Girl or something — the draw
was that strong — and it kind of knocked me out a bit. I almost
felt dizzy. But perfectly alert, like my body was hypersensitive
to every atom of air and particle of sun that surrounded us.
Then I looked at his lips, wondering what it would be like to
kiss the beautiful line of his mouth.

Then he said he doesn't know, but maybe at the Bridge?
Was I there the other night? He thought he recognized me.
There aren't too many girls, he said to me, with silver hair. On
the dance floor?

So I nodded and replied, somewhat demurely: Yeah, I was
there. And I loved the game of pretend we were playing. Because
we both knew we had seen each other before. And the space
between us became even more charged, more exquisite.

Then he told me how much he loved the DJ. Yeah, I said, DJ O'dysseus is a true magician. Then he asked me if I knew him and I said yeah, he's a good friend. Then there was a pause and I said I had been seeing his work around town. Was he new to the city? TNT looked down and nodded. Yeah, he said, he just got here a few weeks ago. That he was living with his dad. That he's just getting to know where all the cool places are now. Meeting some of the right people. He flashed me a sly smile then asked me if I write too. So I tell him. I can't help it. I want him to know who I am, too.

I'm Aura, I said, and I put my hand out, and he did this thing like he bounced off a trampoline and said, No way! You're Aura? Man, I so dig your work. And of course I melted a little here. Because it's so cool that he knows my work. So I told him I'm deeply touched. Which I was. So meaning it. Then I told him his pieces are pretty hot, too. Asking if he'll pardon the expression.

Then he did this kind of shy oh-golly-gee but totally sweet badass swagger and I laughed softly at him and our eyes met again and I thought, *this boy is going to get me into some serious trouble if I don't walk away now*, but I just couldn't. It just seemed like everything in the universe had conspired for us to be together. And I was not about to turn my back on that. So I kept talking to him.

I told him to be careful about getting up. Where the good walls were. What business owners were sympathetic to writers. Where to get spray. And which nights DJ O'dysseus spun wax at the Bridge. Then he asked about who else was in the scene. Who was who. I hesitated telling him that I was in the G7 but mentioned our name as *the* crew out there. He said he had seen the work. That he was really impressed. How it had real presence. I wanted to ask him if he'd seen any work by Story. Or if he'd heard of The Ten or the Kalpa Path. But I didn't want to scare him off with my obsession. Not yet.

So I asked him what scene he had come from and he told me humbly about his adventures. I noted his large hands. That he was a lefty, the residue of black spray stuck on his left forefinger. I listened to his every word, breathless, winding a watch in my brain that could hardly wait for the time when I would see him again.

And then there was a lovely silence between us and I smiled at him again and said how great it was to meet him. And that I hoped I would see him again. At the Bridge. And then he said how great it was to meet me and that he'd definitely go back to the Bridge to see DJ O'dysseus.

And me.

And I thought oh, how perfect is that. TNT. That he should be the one.

To ignite my heart; to feed the spirit of my soul; to burn with the explosion of love.

XIV.

When he came back to the Ryder, Thom decided he was going to check out Winston's library. As he approached the common room, he heard the sound of three voices.

Yo, brother, what'you gonna drink tonight?

Nothing but the real thing, man.

You wouldn't know the real thing if it sat on your face —

Now don't be saying that. 'Cuz you know it ain't true. I had plenty of the real thing. And not from no machine either. Unlike you.

There was silence, then the sound of a solid *ca-thunk*.

Ooo-eee, feel the chill!

Then laughter.

As Thom turned the corner into the room, sure enough, there was Tariq, Duke, and Ray, their backs turned, laughing, gathered around the soda machine. As soon as they saw Thom, they turned around and smiled.

Yo yo yo, if it ain't the new Ryder, right here. In the house!

Thom smiled awkwardly. Hey, he said, stepping forward to give each of them a fist bump.

Your shift just ending? Ray said.

Yeah, Thom answered.

You crewing with Captain D? Tariq said.

Thom nodded.

He's the worst, man, Tariq went on. Seriously. I was so damn happy when I stopped doing commserv. Now I got me a real job.

Where's that? Thom said.

The chilliest place in Buff City, my friend. The Northern Lights Ice Company. So cool it's just cold, if you catch my drift.

This immediately made Duke launch into the lyrics of Vanilla Ice's "Ice Ice Baby," accompanied by Ray's mouth-box rendition of Queen's "Under Pressure" sample: Quick to the point, to the point no faking / I'm cooking MCs like a pound of bacon —

Would you brothers cut that shit out? Tariq pleaded.

Thom looked down and laughed, unable to stop himself.

Tariq put his hand on his hip and basked in Ray and Duke's cover. Uh-huh. Don't you know it. Goddamn Mr. Cool, that's right. That's me.

Duke and Ray went on, unabated, their voices muffled with laughter. Ice ice baby —

You bitches can make fun of me all you want but it beats buffing any day. Especially with Captain D. He's a mean muthafucka.

Ray and Duke stopped and rallied around Tariq, looking at Thom.

It's true, Ray said to him, I'll never forget when I first got here, I went out on crew with him and we were all doing our thing, and me and Duke were buffing this big-ass blockbuster down by the river —

Yeah, Duke interrupted, just like we were supposed to, and Captain D, like, totally *freaked* on us.

Why? Thom asked.

They both shrugged.

Dunno, Ray said. I guess we just weren't doing it right. Whatever, he was just an asshole, you know?

Yeah, Thom replied. I know what you mean.

There was a sense of camaraderie in the air between them.

What'you doing in here? Tariq asked him.

I just came in to check out Winston's library, Thom replied.

He fully expected the three of them to start howling, but instead they looked at him and nodded their heads in solemn approval.

Word, Tariq said. There's some good shit in there. There's even some recorded books, you know? In case you just want to listen. Or if you, y'know, can't read.

Cool, Thom replied. Thanks.

He walked toward the bookshelves of Winston's library, wondering what he might find. As he scanned the shelf, the voices of the others were drowned out as his eye immediately hooked onto one title: *The Collected Poems of William Blake*.

He remembered Driscoll's words and slid the book out of its position on the shelf.

On the cover was a tiger, twisting above a sea of flames.

XX.

I wake up in the middle of the night, sweating. I've been dreaming.

About her. Again.

About finding The Ten. Again.

Except this time something happened. Something that never normally happens. He is in the dream with me.

TNT.

He's holding my hand and leading me through a forest, through a dark tangle of trees. We're running, following a trail that winds through the darkness. And that's when I hear the train. I try to tell him that this is how it begins, with the sound of the train, and that we have to go back, that she's waiting for us. That she's going to show us where The Ten are. But he doesn't understand what I'm saying and he holds my hand tighter.

I look up and we're in a dark, narrow corridor, trees surrounding us on all sides, a ceiling of stars above our heads. And I know, for some reason, that this night she will tell us where to look and I try to pull away from him, telling him I have to go find the Kalpa Path, but he says that this is the path and that there's nowhere else for us to go. And that's when I realize where we are: standing on a train track in the middle of the woods. The silver rails gleam at my feet. And the sound of the train gets closer. And I say to him we have to go. Now. That the train is coming. But TNT just stands there with a strange smile on his face.

This is it, he says to me again. This is the Kalpa Path.

And I want to believe him, I really do. But I know what happens when the train comes. I know what happened to Story. So I pull my hand away and beg him to come with me, and I'm standing there, screaming, but he can't hear me because the train is getting closer and closer, louder and louder.

So I let go. And I can still feel his hand slipping out of mine, the look of surprise in his eyes.

And just before it comes, I wake up.

The rumour is Story started The Ten when she was only fourteen. As far as I know, the rest of her work has been buffed. But The Ten are out there somewhere. It's just no one knows where. If Chef knows — about where The Ten are, or where Tiger Mountain and the Kalpa Path are — he's not saying.

He would be the only one of anybody in the city to know. Since he and Story were like Bonnie and Clyde, the Utah and Ether of the scene. They met at a party when she was fifteen, and from the start it was like something out of a book: he had never known anyone like her; she had never met anyone like him. Apparently, according to Queen Mab, it was love at first sight, destiny with a capital *D*, et cetera. From that first moment, they were never seen without each other again. They had a creative partnership: he inspired her; her work exalted him. They tagged the whole city together, creating everything with the knowledge that what they were doing would someday be more important than they were. They were creating a legend.

By all accounts Story was beautiful: tall and slender, with long cinnamon-coloured hair and green, almond-shaped eyes. But she was tough — and favoured wearing black combat boots and vintage leather jackets. She liked classical music and read a lot of poetry and philosophy. Her home life was secret; she never talked about her family or where she came from. But it was evident things were bad, for whatever reason. Chef never knew this side of her, but obviously it was bad enough that one day Story decided to catch out on some train going west. But she never made it. When she tried to jump on she was pulled under and killed instantly.

No one knew where she had gone until Chef learned the story of a teenage girl fitting Story's description being killed on the tracks. But the teenage girl's name, because she was a minor and according to her family's wishes, was never released. So no one, not even Chef, knew Story's real name. Or where she was buried. It took Chef months to recover. He threw himself into building the G7. He recruited Kane, Queen Mab. MC Lee. The DC. Me. And launched a whole new campaign against social injustice. He also implemented The Rule, Queen Mab guessed, so that Chef wouldn't have to bear witness to anyone else being in love the way he and Story had been. And he refused to speak of the accident. Or her, ever again.

XXI.

Thom walked along the rooftop toward the fire escape and the upper patio of the Bridge. Then he stopped. Directly in front of him was a clean brick wall. There were no other pieces he had to go over or around; the wall was totally his. He wasted no time. Immediately, he reached into his backpack and began bombing it, not as complicated as the burner he had previously done, but in the same style and with the same colours. He did it quickly and efficiently, in less than three minutes, almost without even thinking, executing it perfectly. Thom stood back and admired the piece. It was the best he had done yet. He especially liked the 3D shading to the letters, creating a blocky, cubed effect, the red letters filled in with yellow, looking like they were about to explode.

Thom turned around and looked at the Bridge, thinking about how he would make his ascent up the fire escape to the patio. But as he looked up, he saw someone standing there in dark clothes, face shadowed by the lights, looking down at him, watching.

Thom's first impulse was to run. But he knew he couldn't get caught. So he just stood there, immobilized, looking up into the shadows and holding the stranger's gaze, allowing himself to be seen. Thom stared into the shadowed face, unafraid. Finally, after what seemed an eternity, the figure backed away, turning around, into the light. Thom had seen nothing.

Only later, after he had snuck his way into the club as he had done the last time, did Thom hide in the corner of the dance floor, trying to identify who had seen him, studying people's profiles, reading the outline of their faces in the dim light. Crowds of people passing him by. Then he saw her. Aura. Across the room.

She was leaning against a wall, talking to the doorman, her body half-turned to him. Thom had seen him at the Bridge before — he was hard to miss. Thom guessed him to be easily over seven feet tall. He hunched in the doorway, leaning down over her, carefully watching her while looking up every now and then to survey the room.

Then a guy with dark hair and dark eyes — dressed in a black suit, with a black dress shirt— drinking a pint of beer, swaggered toward Aura. The doorman walked away and the guy leaned over her, slipping his hand around her waist. Thom watched as she smiled ingratiatingly, pushing him away. Then she turned around, exposing her bare back. In the half-light, Thom could see a tattoo of black birds spill over her left shoulder and down her spine. He watched the birds' wings collectively moving, flying over her pale skin.

She looked out into the club and met Thom's gaze head-on.

Without hesitation, she smiled brightly at him and waved. Thom watched as the guy followed the direction of her stare. Instantly, he dropped his hand from Aura's waist and threw his beer down his throat in one gulp. He shot a sharp stare back across the room at Thom. Then at someone directly behind Thom.

Oh shit, Thom thought.

As he turned around to make his escape, Thom found himself blocked by the body of the giant doorman. Unsmiling, he looked down at Thom, his arms folded across his chest.

Leaving so soon?

The guy in the suit walked over. Aura beside him.

Hey, man. Hi there. How do you do? he said loudly as he held out his hand. Nice to meet you. I'm The DC.

Thom shook it, not knowing what else to do.

The DC looked at Aura and grinned ruefully. I was just telling the lovely comrade Aura that I don't think I've seen you around before.

Aura looked at The DC and rolled her eyes. Please. Don't do this. Not here. Not now.

Thom stared at him. There was something familiar about him. But he didn't know what.

The DC shrugged his shoulders and smiled mischievously, his dark eyes flashing Thom a condemning stare. What? he slurred to Aura. I'm just introducing myself —

Just what the fuck do you think you're doing? she said to him, her voice seething with anger. You know he doesn't know, Aura pleaded with him. You're just making things difficult.

The DC smiled again. Know about what? He paused artfully. *Us?*

Exasperated, she looked at The DC, then nervously at Thom, her face flushed with panic.

Don't be so stupid, she answered him. You know exactly what I'm talking about. *He doesn't know.*

The DC laughed again. Thom stood there, hemmed in by the doorman and The DC, wondering what Aura was talking about.

Well, I've seen what he can do, The DC asserted. I've already told Chef about him. And I know he would love to meet the new knight on the scene: That's right. TNT. In the house. Chef's not the only one to recognize talent when he sees it, you know.

Thom felt like he was being sucked away into a black hole. Because he realized, finally, who The DC was, and where he had seen him before. It had been him. The one who had seen him on the rooftop, bombing the wall.

Kane, The DC said, addressing the doorman behind him, could you see that our special guest is escorted to the Library? Then Thom watched as The DC took Aura's arm and led the four of them across the floor to a back door that led to a stairwell.

As they all climbed up the old, darkened stairs, Thom watched Aura plead with The DC. Please don't do this, she said. You know what will happen.

With Kane hulking behind him, Thom could only watch as The DC pulled Aura's arm closer to him in an unrelenting grip. He wondered what the hell was going on when they came to a door at the top of a landing. The DC took some keys from his pocket, inserted one into a lock, and opened the door.

Suddenly, it was very quiet, even though the floor underneath them pulsated with the heavy, luscious beat from downstairs. The air had a peculiar smell that Thom could not identify: stale; rarefied; old. But sweet and strangely sour. Thom followed The DC and Aura; behind him, Kane bolted the door and locked it from the inside. Where was he being taken?

Thom strained to peer into the darkness; his eyes followed a strip of white Christmas lights snaked along the floor. The ceilings stretched high up, casting their shadows across the dilapidated walls. In the distance was a room awash in soft white light. He could hear voices, laughter. The DC kept his arm wound tightly around Aura and looked back at Thom, smirking. Kane urged him on.

As they walked toward the light, Thom looked off into the small, darkened rooms that branched off the main hallway. At one time, the Bridgewater had been a hotel, and these had been its rooms. Now they were used for nothing but garbage. In the cold wash of neon light from the street he could see junked toilets, used carpet, old cabinets, chairs. He could see holes in the walls, panes of broken glass. Graffiti. It was as if he had been pulled into a place where time had stopped: a wormhole where history was irrelevant, where past, present, and future had mutated into the unlikely now.

When Thom reached the end of the hallway and walked into the room, the first thing he noticed was the books. Walls and walls of them, crammed into a multitude of shelves and on the floor in piles, stacked in various heights up to the ceiling. Thom felt the slow, palpable decay of their pages, the mass presence of their power. So that was what he had smelled. In the middle of the room were a group of people sitting in various lounge chairs. He met the eyes of a few of them, recognizing no one.

In the corners of the room were a number of vintage floor lamps, their naked bulbs burning bright. The room filled with sound from the street, the large windows thrown open, letting the hot, humid summer air drift in.

Standing in front of the shelves, his back turned, was a young man wearing a grey t-shirt with the words *You Know You Should / But You Don't* across the back of his shoulders, his head bent down over an open book. Thom recognized him instantly. It was the young man who had worn the white suit. With the eye patch. Thom watched him as he lifted a page from the book in his hands, the distinct flick of his fingers lifting the leaf of the page and turning it over.

Hey Chef, The DC said. Got someone here I want you to meet. This is TNT.

Chef lifted his head and closed the book in his hands and turned around slowly and elegantly. He looked at Thom curiously, as if he were viewing a rare artifact, a perfect pool of white light reflecting in the shiny black satin of his eye patch.

Dynamite, the young man said to Thom, smiling. How do you do? I'm Chef BS. The DC's already told me so much about you. I'm glad you could join us. He bowed slightly. Welcome to the Library at the End of the Universe!

Chef eyed Thom carefully. Do you read?

Thom shrugged. Of course, he replied.

Good. Because you should. If you want to be a real writer. If you want to understand language. Learn its power. Chef raised the book in his hands. *The Revolt of the Masses* by José Ortega y Gasset, he said. Have you read it?

No, Thom answered nervously.

Chef smiled.

Me neither, he confessed. Not until today. But listen to this. He cracked open the book and read: "What I affirm is that there is no culture where there are no standards to which our fellowman can have recourse. There is no culture where there are no principles of legality to which to appeal. There is no culture where there is no acceptance of certain final intellectual positions to which a dispute may be referred. There is no culture where economic relations are not subject to a regulating principle to protect interests involved." Chef paused and looked up at Thom. He noted that everyone else in the room had gathered around them, listening with fascination.

But it's this last phrase I found particularly interesting, Chef continued. "There is no culture where aesthetic controversy does not recognize the necessity of justifying the work of art."

Chef closed the book shut with a soft snap and stared at him.
Do you agree, TNT?

Thom looked at Chef, his heart pounding. He tried not to
stare too much at his eye patch, but he couldn't help it. He'd
actually never seen anyone wear one that wasn't part of a Hallo-
ween costume. Thom looked at Aura, her face brimming with
nervousness.

Well, Thom said, it is rather relevant to what we do, as writers.
Just because graffiti is controversial doesn't diminish the act of
doing it. Or the work itself.

As he smoothed his thin blond goatee, Chef smiled warmly
at Thom. I have other titles you might be interested in if you'd
like to explore our collection.

Come, Chef said, extending his arm to Thom. Let me show
you.

XXII.

One: The DC is a sick, jealous bastard. He introduced himself
to TNT as The DC, which is *strictly forbidden* to all outsiders of
the G7. Unless they want to introduce someone who they feel
would make an important addition to the crew. And so, The
DC, in all his infinite drunkenness, introduced Chef to TNT.

Two: I knew The DC got jealous. But I never knew just how
jealous he could really be. How far he could really go. But tonight
of all nights, he goes outside on the patio at the Bridge and he
just happens to see TNT doing a tag — I mean, what kind of
freaky coincidence is *that*? — and then he sees me talking with
TNT and he loses it.

Three: He puts everything together in his mind. All the details
of the time we did and didn't spend together, and how I said
we had to break up because of the cause (which he used, in the

end, against me) (jerk), and he goes and drinks lots of beer, gets drunk, and schemes this twisted plan so he can get his revenge. Because he knows that if TNT is part of the G7 I have to obey The Rule. Which I told Chef I would do. I promised him. And there's no way I can get away with that kind of mischief twice. And The DC knows it, too. So he goes and spills his guts to Chef about TNT.

Four: Next thing I know Kane and The DC and me and TNT are standing in front of Chef BS in the Library at the End of the Universe and Chef is pulling TNT aside and they're talking low and quietly about philosophy together, and I realize with a kind of vague slippery horror that Chef is taking TNT under his wing.

Which isn't the way it was supposed to happen; which was not the way it was supposed to be. After our beautiful conversation the other day, I had already fantasized what was going to happen. TNT and I would meet at the Bridge by accident and drink and dance and flirt outrageously with each other all night until we staggered back to a park, where we would play tag and make out until dawn before falling asleep in each other's arms under an elm tree.

I feel like screaming. All-out, veins bulging. Because I know I can't do anything. It's too late. All I can do is stand there as Chef announces that we are going to go to Io. And that TNT will be invited as our guest of honour.

At this point, I am holding it together so well that no one in the room even suspects that the only thing I want to do is crawl into a corner of the room and cry. I want to say *He's mine, I found him.* But I can only hold my head up and stare at what appears to be a bonding kinship between TNT and Chef BS as they continue talking together, TNT nodding his head up and down at Chef, mesmerized. My heart is pounding in my head with a kind of white hate and all I want to do is take TNT's hand and run out of the room and beat the crap out of The DC. But I can't do either. And I can't escape. Because Kane stands by the doorway, immovable in stone. And as I watch TNT become enchanted under Chef's spell, The DC turns and looks at me and blows me a kiss and smiles, smiles, smiles.

XXIII.

At the river's edge, Thom followed Chef's footsteps along an invisible path, staring up ahead at the thin, shifting shadow of his body as it led him through the darkness. Thom tried to keep track of where he was going, but as Chef made myriad turns — this way, then that way — he became so disoriented that he had no hope of knowing where he was being taken. All Thom knew was that it was a place called Io.

His eyes adjusted to the pissy yellow light of evening from the city's glow. In the darkness, the river moved molten black beside them, trickling over rocks and stones, meandering into the unknown wilderness of the inner city. Finally, they came into a field, in between the river and the edge of a forest.

As Chef turned around, Thom met his calm, authoritative stare. Behind him were The DC and Kane, DJ O'dysseus, Queen Mab, MC Lee. And Aura. Unsure of what was going to happen, or what he had agreed to do, all Thom knew was that somehow he had been invited to join the G7.

Chef thrust a bottle of whisky into Thom's hand.

Go on, he said, take a hit. Your turn.

Thom lifted the bottle to his lips and took a drink, the clear liquid hot as a match striking his lips, blazing a line of fire down the back of his throat. When he pulled the bottle away, he shuddered involuntarily and passed the bottle back to Chef

BS. He laughed quietly and took a long drink before passing it around. A distant train passed by, and together they all whooped and hollered into the night sky, shouting out as it crashed through the dark.

The G7, Thom was beginning to understand, was no ordinary crew. They were smart. Cool. A kind of bizarre royalty where Chef BS held court, leading the political and intellectual discourse. Everything, from their aliases to their clothes to their signature protests and graff style, pointed to the design of Chef BS. Chef's exertion of power and influence over the G7 was a gregarious kind of Social Darwinism, where each of them vied for his attention, his approval, his respect. There was just something about him. Thom couldn't say what it was. Chef BS was just one of those magical people whom you couldn't help but be drawn to.

As they walked through the trees, it was very quiet. They were in a forest. Thom looked up through the black canopy of branches, seeing studs of hard white stars peep through.

Then, suddenly, Thom heard a sound. It was moving fast through the forest, toward them. Trampling over leaves and branches. A large animal. Before Thom knew what was happening, a dog leaped out of nowhere and crouched down on all fours before him, growling.

It was large, with long, coarse grey fur that stuck up along the scruff of its neck, with big pointed ears and long pointed teeth. Its body was long and skinny, with a great bushy tail. Two yellow eyes with pure black pupils stared wildly at him. Snarling through its clenched jaws, it continued growling at Thom, baring its large teeth.

Kierkegaard, Chef ordered. Enough.

At hearing Chef's voice, the dog sat up at attention, sought the location of his master's hand, and came to sit obediently at his side.

He's part wolf, Chef said to Thom, stroking the dog on the
chin. I found him as a puppy, with a broken foot, abandoned
in a forest. I was reading Søren Kierkegaard at the time.

Thom stared as the dog nuzzled its large, wet black nose into
Chef's hand.

Now he comes and goes when he wants, Chef continued.
These are his woods now, anyway.

Thom watched as the dog studied him intently, its large eyes
flashing over him. It growled again.

I said *enough*, Chef said.

The dog quieted down. Chef tilted his head and looked at
Thom.

He doesn't like you, Chef said.

Thom swallowed, clearing his throat, trying to appear calm.
But he couldn't think clearly. The booze had gone to his head.
And he hadn't foreseen his cover being blown by a wolf.

Maybe he just doesn't know me, Thom replied. Yet.

Chef stared at Thom in the darkness, scrutinizing his face.

Maybe, Chef answered him. Maybe.

As they walked further into the darkness of the woods, Thom
saw some blue LED lights in the distance: tiny and hard and
bright, hanging around what appeared to be, incredibly, a
small silver trailer. As they came closer, Thom immediately
saw the solar panels and the antenna on the roof of the trailer:
the source of Chef's power. Around the trailer was a large
collection of various bicycle frames and bicycle parts scat-
tered in different piles in various states of repair. This was
what, Chef would tell him, among other things, he did to make
money. Upcycling bicycles to create one-of-a-kind machines.
He refused to participate in any economy other than the
one he could create on his own. Which he was. He had left

home when he was eighteen and never went back.

Thom watched Queen Mab and DJ O'dysseus follow Chef inside the trailer, while Kane moved toward a fire pit where there was a circle of chairs, in different shapes and sizes, positioned around it. MC Lee draped herself in a gold satin wingback chair and flashed Thom a hazy smile.

I don't know about you, she said, giggling, throwing one long leg over the arm, but I'm positively s-m-a-s-h-e-d.

Thom watched Kierkegaard circle the woodpile. Out of earshot, he could see The DC and Aura arguing in the darkness of the woods. Thom still didn't understand exactly what had happened. But he had a pretty good idea. Thom stared at them, reading the space between their bodies. They had been lovers. That was obvious, Thom thought. Unable to look away, his jealous mind skidded over their intimacies.

The DC turned and looked at Thom. Then he turned back to Aura and leaned forward, trying to kiss her. Furious, Aura lashed out at him with her fists and pushed him away. The DC stood back and looked at Thom and grinned. Thom quickly turned his head and looked away into the blackened fire pit, a funnel of confusion whirling within him.

He's a real piece of work, The Decameron, MC Lee said flatly, lighting a cigarette and exhaling a blue cloud of smoke. Just like the book he's named for. Fucking epic.

From a small set of speakers outside the trailer came a crackling sound of vintage vinyl. Then a warped distortion of synthesized harpsichords. The entire forest seemed transformed.

DJ O'dysseus emerged from the trailer. His movements were as fluid as the music he played, as if he were always walking on water. He ceremoniously bowed before MC Lee and kissed her hand, then turned to Thom.

Hey man, he said to TNT, offering his hand in a handshake.

Sorry we didn't get introduced. I'm DJ O'dysseus.

Hey, Thom said, reaching out. TNT. Great to meet you. I love your stuff.

Thanks, DJ O'dysseus replied. I love your stuff, too. He sat down on what appeared to be a black piano bench.

What are we listening to? Thom asked.

My remix of the *Clockwork Orange* soundtrack, DJ O'dysseus replied with a smile. Trippy, right?

Melenky Alex is absolutely my favourite fictional bad boy, MC Lee said blithely.

The DC emerged from within the trees and stood at the edge of the fire pit, slightly weaving as Kane dropped an armful of logs into the fire like they were matchsticks.

Yo, Kane, The DC called out, falling back into a black leather chair, his eyelids heavy with drunkenness. My man mountain. Is it 420?

Always, replied Kane with a wide smile. Getting stoned in the zone, you know it.

He sat down in an enormous chair shaped out of a tree trunk and produced a pipe from his pocket. Thom watched as he pushed a giant bud into its bowl and lit it, inhaling deeply, passing it to The DC. Then MC Lee and Thom.

Chef BS and Queen Mab stepped out from the trailer. Thom was still in awe of how small Queen Mab was. She looked like a child, with her tiny arms and legs, her large head perched on her small shoulders, waves of honey-coloured hair trailing down her back. Only her eyes revealed her true age. They were dark and knowing, with a sullen, penetrative stare. She walked around the circle, looking like she was flying, chanting some incantation, then stepped forward and started the fire with a small bundle of papers before sitting in a thatched straw chair next to MC Lee.

Thom watched Chef BS slowly saunter toward a throne
chair made of cut glass with a red velvet seat. He sat down,
slouching, crossing his legs, brooding into the fire. Thom
noticed there were two chairs left. One was made of tubular steel;
the other was a white swivel chair that looked like a distorted
egg cup.

Where's Aura? Chef asked.

Here, a voice said.

Aura emerged from the woods and made her way toward the
circle, taking her place in the tubular steel chair in between Chef
BS and The DC.

In the glow of the blue lights, everything seemed to swim
before him. Even the flames of the fire floated, flickering in blue
air, in undulating orange waves. Chef's cut-glass chair aglow as
he sat enthroned with his one eye like some intergalactic pirate;
the smoke of MC's cigarette and Kane's pipe playing tag in
the air that DJ O'dysseus had orchestrated. He thought of the
tattooed ships he had seen on O'dysseus's arm; Queen Mab's
weird magic. Aura's eyes. The booze and dope tossed inside his
body and mingled together like two concurrent waves.

But he felt strange. Exhilarated. Free.

And nothing, Thom realized, could have prepared him for
this moment. Because everything O'Brien had told him about
the G7 had been wrong. All the information O'Brien had was
based on rumours and half-truths; bad surveillance and shitty
informants.

What O'Brien wanted was facts. Hard evidence. But the G7
was pure fiction. Everything they did existed in an imaginary
realm, even though it was targeted at the mechanisms of the
real world. Which made it, interestingly, even more dangerous.
The G7 belonged to no one except each other. They operated
in their own world, within their own dimension. They did not

participate in society in the way that everyone else around them did: they shifted time and space, creating their own story, together.

Theirs was a kingdom of invention, composed of pure story, myth, and legend. They had never been caught because there was nothing to catch. How could O'Brien persecute an act of imagination?

Thom watched as Kierkegaard circled the fire and approached him.

Tentatively, Thom held out his hand. The long snout of the dog moved instinctively toward Thom's hand. His heart was beating wildly. The dog burrowed his nose in his palm and sniffed, then coolly licked his hand. As he looked down, he met the dog's trusting eyes: their piercing wolf-like glare.

Kierkegaard, Chef BS summoned. Here.

The large dog trotted over to Chef's side and sat by his chair before lying at his feet in the warm light of the fire. There was a reason why Chef BS had such a dog, Thom realized. And it wasn't just for companionship.

Chef BS looked at everyone sitting around the fire and then nodded at Thom.

Please, join us, he said with a motion of his hand. There's a chair beside you.

XXIV.

I am taking the day off. It's decided. No going to the Ridgeway for me today. I called MC Lee this morning and told her. I'm sick, I said, and she said, after last night? Of course you are. Me too. Then she laughed and I said, No, it's true. The last thing I want to do is work with The DC, watching me as he stands behind the line, merrily chop-chop-chopping away.

Because I just know I'd go into that kitchen with my drink tray on my hip and my breath held hostage in my throat and I'd be watching him at his cutting board and I'd be thinking *that's me, that's me, that's me, that's me again,* all those little pieces of my heart being chopped up while he'd just be smiling that sick little demented smile of his. I know I would just lose it and I'd start throwing glasses at him, one by one, watching them fly pretty as crystal birds through the air before smashing on the floor.

I hate him. I can't believe I ever kissed him. That I wanted him to kiss me. That we — gasp, ugh — rolled, pressed (him: hard and me: wet) — double gasp, double ugh — against each other on the grass together like two Hollywood heavyweights in a Big Love Scene. Oh. The. Tragedy.

To think that I tried last night (stupidstupidstupid) talking to him about how I felt. Big mistake. I thought since he said he cared so much for me that he would listen. But he didn't care. He just ignored me and in a big drunken fog went for my face and tried to kiss me in front of everyone. Hallelujah Chef was in his trailer at the time. I got so angry I pushed him away, but then he just laughed. Sick prick. The worst part is that I know TNT saw everything.

What he must think of me. I didn't have the chance to talk to him. All night. About anything. Chef kept him close to his side, testing him. Doing all the things he did to me when I first joined the G7. Making sure Kierkegaard had a good sniff, sharing the whisky, walking to Io through the woods, the selection of the chair — all the rituals of initiation to the G7.

The only real time I got to spend with him was at the end of the night, when we all walked back from Io. As I followed TNT through the field I could see the strong line of his neck. Smell his sweet whisky scent. He was both stoned and drunk

from taking tokes from Kane's pipe and sipping whisky fireside
with Chef BS, and every now and then he stumbled as he walked,
laughing and tripping over his feet, falling into the field. How
I longed to lead him astray, away from the others, pulling him
down into the grass. O I would not utter a single sound. I would
fill my mouth with his silence, make him take all of mine.

Now our whole relationship will be predicated on our mutual
involvement in the G7. We will communicate with each other
now the way all the members do. Via symbols, cryptic messages,
codes. And we will have to obey The Rule. Which, if he doesn't
know anything about it yet, he will. Which is exactly what The
DC wanted. Because if he can't have me, then neither can TNT.

XXV.

When Thom finally returned to the Ryder, it was almost dawn.
His head pounded. He walked quietly down the hallway, gingerly
opening the door to his room, and found a message waiting
for him on a folded slip of paper. There was no name, just a
number, and an instruction to call back.

Thom stepped back out into the hallway, trying not to wake
anyone, and walked into the kitchen where he quietly picked
up the phone and dialled the number. Thom looked at the clock
on the wall. In the dim light, he could barely read the numbers,
but he was fairly sure they said 4:58 a.m. He was so tired. And in
less than three hours, he was supposed to be going out with
Driscoll again.

The phone rang and rang.

Hello? said a voice. Finally. It was a man's. Urgent. Angry
somehow. O'Brien. Of course. It had to be O'Brien.

It's me, Thom said. I got your message.

Have you made contact yet?

Yeah. Tonight.

Good. Tell me what you know.

As Thom struggled to tell O'Brien what he knew — about the members of the G7, the Bridge, the Library, Io — he thought he could hear someone walking down the hallway. Thom stared into the darkness.

Is Winston treating you right? Thom heard O'Brien say.

Thom paused, wondering what he should say.

Yeah, he's been all right, Thom answered. But my crew leader is an asshole.

Thom searched the shadows, his eyes casting over a book-shelf, a table, chairs. Then he thought he saw something, or someone, move toward the kitchen. Panic pounded in Thom's chest. His mouth went slack.

I can't talk now, Thom whispered urgently. I have to go.

Thom hung up the phone and sat in the darkness of the sitting room, listening, his ears pricked. Sure enough, a shadowy figure moved into the room and flipped on a switch. A blast of icy white fluorescent light filled the room.

Tariq stood there in an oversized Tupac t-shirt and sweat-pants, staring at Thom.

Yo, man. Wassup? You couldn't sleep?

Thom nodded. Yeah. Insomniac, that's me.

Tariq yawned and stretched his arms. Not me, man, I gotta sleep or else I get real mean. Besides, I'm on the early shit, I mean — did I say that? — *shift* this morning. They got Ryders coming and going in and out of that place all the time, man. Tariq glanced at the clock. Blast it. I gotta move it. But these bones just won't get into the groove with it.

Tariq's impromptu rhyme sounded like something Kane might say, but sleep was all Thom could think about. More than anything, Thom needed sleep.

Thom went to his room and pulled the curtains against the dawn. He set his alarm, trying to forget he only had three hours before he had to face Driscoll. He dreaded the thought of working. Already the day was blistering, and the sun wasn't even up. Exhausted, Thom crashed in his bed and shut his eyes, his head thundering with all the events of the past evening. He thought of how Kane and The DC had dropped Thom off in the middle of nowhere, on a suburban side street.

The less you know about us, the less we know about you, The DC had said. But the more you know about us, the more we know about you.

Thom was to meet them again, two nights from now, on the river trail, at 9:30 p.m., by the park bench that had the tag *Invincible* on it. The DC had smirked at him, full of easy hatred.

Then he thought of Chef, Io, and Kierkegaard. DJ O'dysseus, Queen Mab, MC Lee. And Aura. When he'd walked back through the field, she had been there with him. He wanted to pull her away from the group, take her into the trees, into the forest, away from all of them, away from The DC. But he had no choice. Chef BS had kept him close. And whether he was ready or not, Thom — officially or unofficially — was a part of the G7.

Thom saw Chef's face float up before him, the blur of his eye patch. He was the undisputed leader. And though he seemed older than any other member, there was something boyish about him. Thom wanted to know as much about him as he could. As he drifted off to sleep, he recalled the strange story that Chef had shared with them that night around the fire. It was about three girls who were buried in the snow and saved by a boy — a boy who died and was miraculously reborn, resurrected in the stars.

Three short hours later, the alarm went off. Thom's eyes shot wide open. It was like he had just closed them. He didn't even remember sleeping. Later, when he was in the truck with Driscoll, Thom tried to remember the events of the story that Chef had told, but he could only remember bits and pieces of the tale. Absentmindedly, he stared into the middle distance, sleep a distant landscape he had no hope of reaching until that night.

For their first site visit that morning, Driscoll dragged Thom out to a remote area along the river where there was a wall backing onto a concrete factory. The entire wall was covered with layers of graff. It would take them hours to do it. Thom felt sick at the prospect of the work that lay ahead. He stared into his paint tray with remorse, feeling like he was going to be sick.

What time did you go to sleep last night? Driscoll asked him, noting his behaviour. You look like shit.

Thom stared at the wall and rolled up without looking at Driscoll.

Late.

Driscoll took a long drink of water from the stainless steel bottle. They really work you at that Ryder, huh?

Thom turned and looked at Driscoll.

No, only you do, motherfucker.

Driscoll laughed and smirked at Thom.

That may be. But I do it for your own good. I'm supposed to do more than make you work hard. I want you to learn — no, I want you to *know* — that graffiti is vandalism and that vandalism is a violation of public property and that vandalism is not just wrong, *it's against the law.*

Thom took a deep breath. The sun burned at his back. He felt dizzy he was so tired. He felt like telling him to fuck off.

I know, he replied, irritated. I know. But look at this. Thom stepped back and pointed at the wall. I mean, *really*. Look at this. This, this ... wall. As soon as we buff over it, it's not even a wall anymore! You know what it is? It's an open invitation. A *provocation*. To write more. I see walls like these, and I think *fuck you, I'm going to bomb that*. You can't make me stop writing. You can't silence me or stop my creativity! I mean, so really, what's the fucking point? The more we paint over these stupid walls the more writers keep writing. They don't care! They don't give a shit! So why should we?

Driscoll looked at Thom and smiled. Then he put his hands together and began to clap, very loudly and slowly.

Congratulations, bad boy. You just passed the first step.

What the fuck are you talking about? Thom said angrily.

Recognizing that graffiti isn't about art, but about power.

Don't patronize me, Thom said. I know what graffiti is about.

Do you? Because all I hear you talking about is freedom of creative expression. That's bullshit. Graffiti is a way of sticking it to the man. Exactly like you said. Of saying *fuck you*. Of rebelling against society. Because if you were really interested in your creativity, you'd be working your ideas out in a sketchbook, or on paper and canvas, like any other real artist. You wouldn't care whether it was on the side of a bridge, or a train, or a building. You wouldn't, like you said, give a shit.

Thom looked at Driscoll with hatred. He couldn't believe he had been a writer. And Everest, no less. Thom had so much he wanted to say, but he just couldn't find the right words. He felt himself slipping off into some dark, miry corner, tempted by Driscoll's evil, twisted logic.

Being in the public domain is exactly what makes graffiti art, Thom slowly struggled to say. It has no audience in a sketchbook, or in some art gallery where no one will ever see it. That only serves some elite audience.

Ever heard of Jean-Michel Basquiat? Driscoll said.

Fuck you, Thom said. Fuck you.

Oh, that's poetic, Driscoll said. Very original.

Thom's brain surged with fury. He realized, instantly, that he was having the same kind of argument with Driscoll that he used to have with his father. It was part of the reason he'd had to leave. During the whole time he was growing up, Thom's father had constantly belittled him and his opinions, telling him that while he was living in *his* house he had to live under *his* rules, and he never let Thom forget it. Driscoll was just the same. And just like his father, Driscoll refused to understand his point of view or listen to any of his opinions — never mind think about his feelings.

What about the G7, then? Huh? Thom said. They use graffiti as a way to combat power — using slogans and phrases and popular images to turn people's impressions of power upside down. You know, the way they use stencils and prefabricated images and lettering? Like Banksy. Their graffiti is real street art.

Driscoll scoffed. How the fuck do you know so much about the G7?

I don't, Thom said, backtracking, looking away from Driscoll's penetrating gaze. I just know their work. It says everything about who they are.

Yeah, Driscoll said, determined to have the last word, and nothing, too.

Thom didn't want to argue with Driscoll anymore. He knew he could never win, that Driscoll would never let him. Driscoll took a long drink from his stainless steel water canteen. The void of silence between them filled with the sound of distant traffic.

Where the fuck are we, anyway? Thom said as he swung his head around, trying to get his bearings.

Close to downtown, Driscoll said. The main trail here leads to downtown, and that trail, Driscoll said, indicating a narrow, muddied path that was barely visible through the trees, that path leads to the river. Follow me, I'll show you.

Thom followed Driscoll's lead as they stepped through the line of trees. Within a minute, they were at the river, under a bridge.

Thom looked around. Under the curved cement arch of the bridge, graffiti was everywhere. Against one of the walls was an old sleeping bag, some blankets. A burned-out fire pit. Among the garbage that was strewn everywhere, Thom could see a multitude of beer cans, bottles, and nickel bags.

Thom stared dismally down at the ground, and then looked around again. There was graff everywhere: tags by DSNC, Ceo, and Brass; throw-ups by Down; and stencils by Thesis and Dubble. Driscoll took a swig from his water canteen.

Why did you bring me here?

Because I needed to take a piss, Driscoll said.

Thom surveyed the other side of the bridge. There, on the opposing wall, was a huge blockbuster, straight ahead of him, in full, white block letters: *Story*.

What's that? he said to Driscoll.

Driscoll turned his head to look.

What do you think it is? It's a blockbuster.

Why hasn't it been buffed?

I can't be responsible for cleaning up this entire goddamn city, can I?

Driscoll zipped up and let his words hang in the air. Now let's get back to work, he said. I've had enough of your bullshit for one day.

On the drive back to the Ryder, Driscoll was uncharacteristically silent. Thom looked away and out the window, thinking

again of the large blockbuster of Story. It wasn't the first time
he had seen that name. Thom contemplated asking Driscoll
who Story was, but he decided it would be better to ask one of
the guys at the Ryder. Or some of the G7.

If he could get her to trust him a little bit more, he would
ask Aura. Maybe she would know who Story was.

XXVI.

This morning I woke to my mother calling my name, telling
me it was time to wake up.

I pulled the sheets over my head, trying to ignore her voice.
Aren't you going to work today? she called. *It's already eleven o'clock.*

Oh shit, I thought. I'm late.

I stared up at the ceiling. Just the thought of working at
the Ridgeway made my stomach lurch. But I couldn't get
away with missing another day. And I couldn't ignore The DC
anymore. I could see my mother hesitating on the other side
of the door, her brow ridged with trust, not wondering if
I was in bed — or if I was even home. I was too good a girl to
disappoint them, sadly. I rolled over and scanned my bedroom
floor, locating what I needed to shove into a bag to bring
to work.

I'll be right out, I called back to her brightly, then dragged
myself out of bed.

As I biked through the massive limestone and wrought iron
gates of the Ridgeway and followed the winding, tree-lined road
of asphalt toward the clubhouse, my mouth went dry with a
kind of sick panic.

It happened every time I came here. Every time I looked out
over the vista of the meticulously clipped lawns, the sloping

green fairways in the distance. Every time I saw the clubhouse, with its wide, flat brown roof and glass and steel architectural features. Every time I saw the pool, toilet-water blue, accented by endangered Balinese teak rainforest furniture, artfully arranged around the patio. Every time I saw the tennis courts, with their pairs of players in white shorts and white t-shirts, smashing balls into the invisible air. Every time a stupid golf cart whirred past.

In the restaurant, MC Lee took one look at me and asked me where the hell I had been. She'd been slammed all morning. Sorry, I said. I slept in. MC Lee lanced me with a burning stare.

I wish I could do that, she said. But do you think my parents would ever let me sleep in? No fucking way.

I held off going into the kitchen as long as I could. But the instant The DC saw me walk through the swinging doors from the dining room he was onto me right away. He looked at me hungrily, all big bad wolf, his dark eyes grinning with mischief, shouting out to DJ O'dysseus that the one and only Aura was in the house.

I tried to ignore him as long as I could. But as soon as I placed my order he looked at my chit and said sorry, but we were out of that. And that, in fact, we were out of absolutely everything. That there was no food at all. I looked at DJ O'dysseus, who was walking toward the walk-in cooler. He shook his head at me, mouthing the word *sorry*. I didn't know whether he meant about the food or The DC.

Fuck off, I said to The DC.

He laughed at me and told me he knew this girl once who told him that if you fuck on you get better results. He followed this with a quick, Wanna? Right here? Right now? Then he yelled at DJ O'dysseus to back him up with a beat, and The DC started to rap.

I said how 'bout it? About you and me? I'm talkin'-'bout-the-one-and-only-Aura-and-me — The DC. Yes it's a big bang, a blast of TNT, there's a fire in the kitchen and it's burning in —

DJ O'dysseus and The DC broke off in midstream as Queen Mab and MC Lee entered the kitchen. Mab glared penetratingly at both of us. She knew exactly what was going on. What had gone on. She missed nothing. And she told Chef everything. She looked scornfully at us and walked out.

This is bullshit, MC Lee said. I'm taking my break.

As she walked out the back door, DJ O'dysseus crept silently back into the walk-in cooler, leaving The DC and I standing alone in the kitchen. I knew the reference to TNT had been deliberate — everything with The DC was cryptic, encoded, full of guessing games.

Please don't do this, I said to him.

Do what?

He threw his hands up in the air like he wasn't doing anything.

So then I tell him it's over. That I'm doing it. By The Rule. From now on. For the cause. Like I talked about. That it wasn't him. That it was me. And I needed to dedicate myself to the principles of the G7. Out of respect for Chef. Out of respect for all of us. And that I'd appreciate it if he would give me the chance to do that.

You breaking up with me? The DC laughed awkwardly.

Then, after a moment, he said, of course he would do that. Respect my choice. But it hurt him deeply. He thought we had something real.

He raised his face and looked at me. He wanted me to know he didn't trust TNT. Especially not with me. So he was gonna be watching us.

Real close.

After work, I smoked a bowl of weed with Kane. Then, on my way home, I stopped at the wall where I had first met TNT, disappointed to see that it had already been buffed. My heart sank. It had been so beautiful.

It was a hot summer night, and as the cicadas buzzed in the trees while my head buzzed with hallucinogenic intensity, I pulled my bike off the trail and wheeled it into the trees. I took off my backpack, zipped it open, and pulled out a can of black Rusto I'd stolen out of my dad's "home improvement" corner in the garage. Like he'd ever notice it was gone. Or care. I pinched off the cap and shook the can a couple of times. The sound of the little ball rolling around inside the can never failed to excite me. It was that sound that got me. Every time.

As soon as I depress the grooved tip, everything fades away. All the stupid voices in my head from today. All the bullshit with The DC. Mab. MC Lee. The spot where the paint hits the wall gleams in beautiful glossy black. Like shellac. It only takes a few seconds. And then I'm done. I put the good ol' can o' Rusto back in my bag and hop back on my bike. My heart pounds. And then I get the kick. Pure adrenalin, like water rushing around my ears. No one's seen me, of course. But there's always that risk. Which is what, I admit, I am kinda hooked on. That, and seeing my name. But today I've done something different. Something new I've been working up in my black book. Today just seemed like the perfect day to get it up.

As I speed away, I turn around and look at what I've done, free floating in the middle of the freshly buffed wall, hovering in space. A single phrase, in plain black letters. Easy to read. Plain to see. An homage to TNT. I could still see the words from a distance. They read, simply:

THERE'S DYNAMITE UNDER HERE

XXVII.

When Thom got back to the Ryder, he was surprised by how quiet it was. Normally it was abuzz with guys coming and going from community service and shift work. As he walked alone down the pale grey corridor, Thom passed Winston's office. The quote "We will stomp to the top with the wind in our teeth — George Mallory, 1924" emerged from the photo collage of mountains taped on his office door. Thom wondered what Winston's thing was with mountains. Was there a connection between Driscoll as Everest and Winston's obsession? he wondered.

Thom walked straight toward the kitchen. He needed coffee if he was going to go out again tonight. As he stepped into the small, brightly lit room, he saw Carlos sitting alone in a single chair at the table, a small book laid out before him.

Sensing Thom entering the room, Carlos turned around and nodded, acknowledging him.

Hey man, Thom said.

Hey, Carlos replied, going back to reading his book.

What are you reading? Thom asked.

The Naked Mountain by Reinhold Messner. He was the first mountaineer ever to climb Everest without oxygen. In 1978. How fucking ballsy is that?

You got it from Winston's library?

Of course, Carlos replied. Where else?

What else have you read from there? Thom asked.

Oh, pretty much everything. Literature. Biography. Philosophy. Poetry —

I got a book of poetry out from Winston's library, Thom confessed, interrupting Carlos. *The Collected Poems of William Blake.*

Carlos lifted his eyes from the page and looked at Thom.

Yeah, I read that. I really dig that poem, I think it's called —

"The Tiger?" Thom interjected.

Carlos shook his head. No, no, it's called "Are Not the Joys of Morning Sweeter," or something like that ...

Oh, Thom said, disappointedly. I haven't read that yet.

He didn't want to confess to Carlos that he hadn't even opened the book yet, let alone read anything inside.

I've read some pretty good stuff lately, Carlos continued. Classics, mainly. *The Decameron, 1984 ...*

Thom felt his breath catch in his throat. What did you just say, the de-what? *The Decameron?*

Yeah, Carlos said. I don't know what the big fuss is. It's kind of boring. I think people just like the idea of it more than anything. Or saying that they read it.

Thom nodded, pretending he knew what he was talking about, though all he could think about was what MC Lee had said about The DC's namesake. He stared intently at the book resting under Carlos's palms.

What's with Winston and all the mountain stuff? Thom asked.

I think Winston thinks it's motivational for us juvies, since we won't listen to him or any other authority figure. But we'll respect some dude like Messner. I also think he thinks that if we want to rebel, there are other radical ways to do it.

Like climb a mountain, Thom said.

Basically, Carlos replied.

But there's no mountains around here.

That's why he wants us to climb the mountains of our minds, my friend. Through rehab. Reading. Positive realization. Revelation. You know, the usual shit that happens at the Ryder when you're not whacking off.

Can I look at that? Thom asked.

Carlos shrugged. Yeah, sure, man. Go for it.

He handed Thom the book and leaned back in his chair.

You went out with Driscoll today, didn't you?

Hmmmm, Thom murmured absently, turning over the pages. Bearded men with frostbite seemed to be on every page.

How was it?

Huh? Thom looked down at Carlos. Oh, you know, the usual torture. As he flipped through the pages, Thom could feel Carlos staring at him.

We saw some crazy shit by Down —

Yeah, he got busted a while back. Public mischief. Comm-serv. Probation. You know.

Thom sighed. Yeah. He paused and handed the book back to Carlos. Hey, do you know who Story is?

A slow, sad smile crept over Carlos's face.

It's been a while since Story graced the scene, Carlos said. May she rest in peace.

She's dead?

Yeah. She died trying to catch out on a train. A couple of years back now.

Oh, Thom said quietly, thinking about the piece he had seen with the birds flying out of the book with the words *Story, RIP* underneath.

Driscoll took me to this spot we'd never been before today, under this bridge. Where there was all this graff. And I saw this huge blockbuster, in white. Story.

Carlos smiled and nodded.

Yeah, some say the start of the Kalpa Path is around there somewhere.

The what?

Carlos shifted his head to one side and tilted his head at Thom.

You've never heard of the Kalpa Path? Which leads to Tiger Mountain?

Thom immediately thought of the tiger piece. He shook his head wildly. O'Brien had told him none of this information.

Yeah, apparently there's this masterpiece up at the top of the mountain called The Ten. Totally biblical.

No way, Thom said. Tell me more.

I wish I could, man, Carlos replied. But like I said. I don't really know that much.

Do you know where it is? Thom asked.

Yo, get this. No one knows where it is. Or if it even exists. It's just some crazy-ass rumour that's been out there since she died. And let's face it, if The Ten did exist, they would have probably been buffed. Especially in this fucking town. Carlos paused. The thing is, he continued, there's no way to find out. No one knows anything. And if they do, they're not saying. For some reason, it's, like, super secret. I mean, top.

Thom thought carefully about what Carlos was saying. If what he said was true, there was one person who could give Thom the answers to these questions. And he was right down the hallway.

XXVIII.

Today Chef sent me a message at the Ridgeway through Mab. Said he wanted to see me. Tonight. On my own. At Io. I knew Queen Mab would talk to him about what happened. I was busted. I was going to have to come clean. Tell him everything about me and The DC. And TNT.

I felt nervous walking to Io by myself. Normally, the whole crew of us went. But tonight, I was alone. I could hear the crickets in the grass, see the sunset reflected in the river. It was a silky, humid night. As I passed through the field and entered the forest, I turned around and watched the last bit of blue sky disappear under a brim of pink and red and yellow. Orange hugged the horizon. It was truly beautiful. Sometimes nature just throws up the most radical burner you'll ever see.

As I turned into the darkened woods, I could roughly make out the path at my feet. I knew Kierkegaard would soon be coming to find me, and as I stepped over the fallen logs that marked the entrance to Io, I heard his nimble footsteps approach. His wet nose touched my hand, and he instantly leaned against me, bowing in submission, wagging his tail. I stroked the top of his head affectionately and then followed his lead for the rest of the way.

When I arrived at Chef's trailer, I peered inside and saw him reading a book called *The Illuminatus! Trilogy*. I almost forgot to breathe when I realized he was not wearing his eye patch. For the first time, I saw the indentation of where his eye had been. It looked like a pale pink flap of wrinkled skin; an eyelid sewn shut. Then, sensing my presence, or perhaps Kierkegaard's scratching his foot at the door, Chef calmly put on his eye patch and swung open the door to the trailer. He was shirtless, and I could see the bones of his ribcage, pale and luminescent in the soft blue light. A perfumed trail of musky incense floated up to my nostrils. He looked at me and smiled hazily.

Aura, he said, I'm happy to see you. Please, come in.

I stepped inside, followed by Kierkegaard, who lay down under a small table near the entrance to the trailer. Chef motioned his hand toward the silver bench seating. Then asked me if I wanted some sun tea. He had just brewed some today.

Sure, I said, smiling nervously. "Chef's Own" organic blend was a potent mixture of natural and hallucinatory ingredients. Part peppermint, part green matcha, part sinsemilla, part psilocybin. With fresh lemongrass and fresh lemon balm. And red clover honey.

I watched as he turned around and lifted a glass pitcher off the small kitchen counter and poured us each a tall glass of tea. It was hard to tell how old Chef was. According to Queen Mab, he was twenty, the oldest out of all of us. But sometimes he seemed like he could have been forty. Or fourteen. He had this strange agelessness to him that always struck me as proof of his prophet status.

He handed me my glass. The tea was strong, cold, sweet.

Delicious, I said.

Satisfied, Chef BS bowed, smiling at me as he sat down and raised his own glass and took a long drink. I couldn't help but stare at his lean, hairless torso, his strong, muscular arms. Electronic music pulsed out of the stereo. I looked at the "Now Playing" shelf. It was *The Social Network* soundtrack. Of course. But then again, Chef only ever listened to soundtracks. He believed music should act like a background of sound to accompany the movement of life. Or so DJ O'dysseus told me that's what Chef had told him. When he was chosen as the resident DJ of the G7.

So you wanted to see me? I asked. Chef looked at me sweetly and saintly and said, You tell me. It was exactly the kind of classic, double innuendo, mindfuck kind of thing Chef liked to do. I smiled, then laughed, embarrassed. Well, I began, I wanted to tell you about The DC. And me. And TNT, I said boldly.

Go ahead, he said.

Well, as you know, I started telling him, I am no longer involved with The DC in any way. It is totally over. And I wanted you to know from me, not Queen Mab. Because I really want you to know that I care about the cause and how committed I am to you and the principles and ideas of the G7.

Chef BS laughed lightly. There has never been any question of your loyalty, Aura. Only your self-control.

I smiled at him, my brain ticking. The tea was beginning to take effect. As Chef stretched out his arms along the back of the bench, I couldn't help but stare at his exposed underarms, their tufts of soft blond hair; the dark pink of his nipples. It was hot in the trailer, and I wiped my forehead with the back of my hand. A piercing drone of mosquitoes buzzed outside the screened-in windows.

I knew about you and The DC, Chef said with a mischievous smile, but not about TNT.

So I told Chef about the night we met. And how much I loved his work and that I hoped we could work together. As I spoke, I felt Chef watching me. Even though he only had one eye, his gaze was one of the most penetrating I had ever known. Something about it was all-knowing and pervasive.

Then he told me he was happy I felt this way, because the real reason he wanted to see me was because he wanted me to shadow TNT. To be his eyes, his ears: to find out everything he does. And then show him everything we do.

Chef's words hung in the air. I couldn't believe it. I could never obey The Rule if I had to work beside TNT every night. Not after everything I'd been through with The DC.

What? I said. I can't. I just can't. I suggested The DC, Kane — anyone. Anyone but me would be better suited. Chef listened but said nothing. I told Chef that I was honoured, really, that he would think of me first. But, I confessed, I mean seriously, who's kidding who? I'm not that good. Really. And what about DJ O'dysseus? They totally seemed to hit it off. And he knows all the best walls. Where to get shit. You know? He's totally the one.

But Chef BS just looked at me and smiled a secret, knowing smile. Then he reminded me of what he had just told me. That there was never any question of my loyalty. Only my self-control.

He was considering me — and only me — for something very important.

But why? Why me? I pleaded.

He told me he needed someone he could trust. He didn't expect me to understand right away. But he needed me to do this. And that was all. Reluctantly, I agreed, with the promise not to tell anyone.

Consider this a test, he said. Of your will, if you will. And as a chance to learn the truth. *The truth?* I said.

The truth is always what you least expect, Chef said. Story told me that once.

It was the first time he had ever mentioned her name to me. I knew this would have been a good time to ask him again about The Ten, but I had already tried once before, unsuccessfully, when I first joined the G7. Back then, I didn't know I wasn't supposed to talk about Story or ask about where the Kalpa Path was. But now that he had said her name, I searched for something to say, to see if I could break his silence about her, so I told him my recurring dream about her, in the hope that he might tell me, if he indeed knew, the location of The Ten.

After I told him about the train and Story standing in the street, Chef stared at me piercingly and told me that it was a gift to dream of someone in that way. That it meant that they have a connection that is both within and outside this world, beyond the reality of what we experience. He said the words slowly and clearly for me to understand. Then I asked him if it had ever happened to him. And Chef said yes. When he was younger. A girl. He didn't know what it meant at the time.

Story? I said.

Chef flashed a sad smile.

No. Someone else.

Chef set his glass down on the floor. Kierkegaard sat up

and lurched toward it. In a daze, I watched the animal lick the rim lasciviously. Knowing I was watching, Kierkegaard turned his large grey head and stared at me with his yellow eyes. The tea. My head was swimming with hallucination.

Chef reached across the table and took my hand.

I'm glad you came to see me, comrade Aura, he said. Your dream is a vision. It's given me a sign, one I didn't expect, one that I've been waiting for.

I didn't know what sign he was talking about, but I looked at Chef in a kind of vestal desire, full of awe. My hand was burning.

XXIX.

Thom knocked on Winston's door, but there was no answer. He rested his eyes on a picture on Winston's door of two smiling men sitting side by side on some mountain. Thom studied the picture more carefully, noting the caption below: "Moving down after triumph, Hillary and Tenzing are still united and delighted."

Looking for me?

Thom turned around. Winston stood before him in the hallway and appraised him cautiously.

Yeah, I just had some questions I wanted to ask.

Oh? Winston replied, digging in his pockets for his keys. Questions. Well, then, you better come into my office.

Winston unlocked the door and propped it open with a chunk of rock.

From the foothills of Denali, Winston remarked, indicating to the rock with a nod of his head. Talk about your hand-held luggage. I carried that chunk of mountain all the way from Anchorage. He smiled wistfully. Have a seat, he said to Thom, gesturing to a chair against the wall.

Thom stared at the walls of the small, dark, windowless office. It was more like a prison cell than any of the rooms at the Ryder, but Winston had wallpapered it with pictures of mountains. Winston sat in his black office chair and clasped his hands together.

So what questions did you want to ask?

I want to know where the Kalpa Path is, Thom asked. And how to get to Tiger Mountain.

Winston looked at Thom with a cold, knowing stare. Then he stood up and closed the door, heaving aside the chunk of ashen rock with his foot. The door swung silently closed. Winston sat down again.

Well, Winston began, the first thing you should know is that whoever told you about the Kalpa Path probably doesn't know anything about it. Or Tiger Mountain.

So they're real? Thom said.

Of course they're real, Winston replied. As real as a legend can be.

I don't get it. So they're not real?

No, Winston said. Not really. It's just a story.

But —

Who told you? Carlos? Winston laughed lightly. Carlos reads a lot of books. He imagines many things.

Winston looked sternly at Thom. I'm not supposed to tell you this, but I think O'Brien would want you to know, as an informant, the validity of your sources. Carlos is a total megalomaniac. Did you know that? He's in here on ten counts of identity theft. Not bad for a minor.

Thom looked away in silence.

By the way, I got the supplies you asked for, Winston said. They're in the back of my car.

Oh, Thom said, still thinking about Carlos, thanks.

What about Driscoll?

Winston furrowed his eyebrows at Thom. What about him?

What can you tell me? I have to know, as you say, the validity of my sources. I heard Driscoll was once a writer. And a Ryder too. Is that true?

Winston nodded solemnly. But I'd be careful with what he says, too, Winston said. Now that you've gotten to know him. As a rule, don't trust anyone.

He met Winston's eyes. Behind him, mountain ranges soared, their summits raised behind his head.

Not even you?

I don't know what O'Brien's told you, but I've been doing this for eighteen years. I've seen a lot of you come and go over that time. Only a handful of you make it real. The rest of you are just killing time.

Even though he knew he shouldn't, Thom silently resented the fact that Winston lumped him in with the rest of the other Ryders.

Any other questions? Winston asked.

No, Thom said. Their continuing code of doublespeak had begun again.

Winston stepped forward and opened the door, pushing the hunk of mountain rock against the foot of the door.

The man who removes the mountain begins by carrying away small stones, Winston said elegiacally. See how easy that was? That's all a mountain is. A rock. Just like that one. It doesn't matter how big or small.

Thom looked down at the rock, and remembered what Omar had said about Winston having Everest in his juvie.

One more thing, Thom said. Who is Story?

Just another writer, Winston replied. She died two years ago trying to jump a train.

And what about The Ten?

Pure fiction, he said.

So it's not real?

No, Winston said sadly. She was real. That's the problem. No one wants to believe the truth. And the truth is she's dead.

XXX.

This morning I woke to the sound of blaring sirens, and for a second I thought, *Hurray, they've come to find me!* My heart pounded as I heard them come closer and I imagined the scene as I've imagined it so many times before: my parents getting ready to leave for work, opening the door and saying *Can I help you, officer?* as the cop car sits in the driveway, and the officer looks at both my parents and says *Is your daughter home?* And they say slowly *Yes*, while I, upstairs, have already grabbed my SOL backpack — which, in case of just such an emergency, is packed and ready to go and will get me through three to four weeks in the wild or until I can find my way clear. By the time my mother is calling my name up the sweeping staircase of steel and white carpet I am already gone, slipping free through trees and sunlight, and my parents — who at least one night fucked and forged my D and my N and my A — are speechless, because the good girl that they thought I was is gone. And they look back over all the years of pandering neglect and wonder what the fuck went wrong.

One thing Chef has always taught us is how to have an exit strategy. And as the fantasy played out in my mind, it took me another second to realize that they weren't coming to my house. And that it was an ambulance. On the next street over. My stomach caved with disappointment. I should know by now that I'm never going to get caught. But there's always that chance that I'm going to fuck it up. Get picked up by the cops. Because what I am doing *is* illegal. Which is the thrill. And why I keep doing it.

I can still remember the first piece I did. With a ballpoint pen. On the wall in my bedroom when I was thirteen. My mom found it and for the first time, ever, noticed something I'd done. She freaked out. Like, seriously. I got grounded and everything. She even told my Dad. And we had this long conversation, together, about what a serious thing it was. And how I was to never, ever, do it again.

The next time I used a Sharpie marker. The tag was nothing great. Just some crazy signature I thought I'd try out. I wanted to see if I could do it. If I could be brave enough to try. All these boys were doing it — why couldn't I? I remember being scared shitless. But excited. Looking all around me — trying to see if anyone saw me. Then I just pulled out the marker and just did it. On this footbridge near downtown.

When I was done, and I didn't get caught, I realized it wasn't good enough. I needed to do more. To get my name out there, I knew I would have to do something different. And not just to get other writers' respect — but to make people stop and look. To make my parents angry at me. So that's where the impulse first came to work up corporate billboards and advertising. Just doing tags wasn't enough: I wanted to penetrate the conscious-ness of society, peel back a layer of reality. Which is what I'm still trying to do. But I still can't get caught. And my parents still believe I am the same good girl I always was, that I always will be.

I sat up and looked out the window. As I stared into the sunshine, my head felt like a vacuum: light pouring through it so fast it felt like I was spinning. There was already a haze in the air, thick with heat, heavy and humid. I could hear the cicadas up in the treetops, electric, singing shrilly. I'd heard the news and all the weather people were saying that it was going to be the hottest day of the year. It was an appropriate forecast, I thought, all things considered.

Because tonight I was going out with TNT.

XXXI.

Thom sat on the park bench with the tag *Invincible* by the river, waiting for the G7, just as it had been arranged the first night he met them all at the Bridge. He stared up at a swarm of moths, battering into the streetlamp above him. Thom watched them buzz and drop, staggering back into the darkness and then, drunk with shock, flicker back, propelled by some hidden force, drawn to the light.

Between working with Driscoll during the day and the G7 at night, Thom had hardly any time for himself. Sometimes he woke up so tired at the Ryder that he didn't know who he was. His identity felt fractured, fragile, endangered. But he was getting closer to knowing what he needed to know to tell O'Brien. He could feel the truth, brimming beneath the surface of things.

So he didn't want to make any mistakes he might regret with Aura.

Thom looked down both sides of the trail. Even though the sun had set more than an hour ago, the heat bristled in the darkness around him, so heavy and muggy he felt as if he could swim through it. It had been the hottest day of the summer on record, and still the heat seemed to fumble out of the trees, filling up the air. Tiny rivulets of sweat dripped down his back, collecting at the base of his spine.

Somewhere out there lay the Kalpa Path and Tiger Mountain

and The Ten, he was sure of it. He stood on the bench, teetering on the top edge, looking over the edge of the embankment, further down the trail. Below him, the river pooled and gathered in the soft blackness.

I wouldn't do that if I were you.

Thom turned around, instantly recognizing Aura's halo of short, platinum silver hair. He stared at the lone strap of a black bra underneath her white tank top. The wing of one black bird flying over her shoulder. He jumped down and stood in front of her.

You're late, he said.

Have you been waiting long? she said.

Hours, he said.

She smiled and rolled her eyes.

Seriously, though. Did it take you long to get here?

No, Thom lied. I just — he paused, thinking quickly — you know, walked.

Her face brightened. Oh? You live downtown?

Thom hadn't anticipated that she would ask so many questions. He would have to be more careful than he thought.

No, I took the bus, he said. And then walked here.

Oh, she said.

Where is everybody? he asked.

Aura smiled. Just you and me tonight, homey. The rest of the crew had other plans.

Thom smiled, but immediately knew Aura had been sent alone to check him out.

Think of this like a first date, Aura said. Or something like that. The plan is for us to meet here every night. At the same time, same place. Clear?

Crystal, Thom said.

They walked along the river trail in a complicated silence,

aware of both the desire and suspicion that existed between them, pulling them together, pushing them apart.

The Graffpol buffed your piece, Aura finally said. You know, the one you were doing when we met?

Yeah, Thom said snidely, his mind skipping over the moniker. I know.

Chef says the Graffpol are writers doing community service. For getting caught, you know?

Yeah, Thom answered flatly again, remembering how he felt buffing his own work.

It's so sad, Aura continued.

Thom wasn't sure what Aura was fishing for — if she was fishing for anything; it wasn't clear.

Well, you better be careful then, Thom said to her. You don't want to end up being one of them.

Aura laughed. Like that's ever gonna happen. Not to me, anyway.

It could happen to anyone, Thom said.

Aura laughed again. *I wish*. Besides. I'm too young.

Thom smiled and then feigned a deep voice, pretending to use a microphone, and swung his hand out in front of her. And how old are you?

She flashed her eyes at him. They danced, two blue jewels. They were playing a game of tag. She testing him; he teasing her. Back and forth. Finding out who each other was.

How old do you think I am?

I don't know. Eighteen, nineteen.

Aura dropped her jaw and laughed.

Really? C'mon! Seriously?

TNT shrugged. Why? You're not?

Unh-unh, she said smugly.

So how old are you?

Guess.

She looked at him with a sly, embarrassed smile that made his stomach flip.

I don't know, he laughed. Fourteen?

She threw her hand out in the air, slapping him.

Ha ha, very funny. The smugness was gone, but she was still smiling. I'm seventeen. In five weeks. She paused, then said: Did you really think I was eighteen?

TNT nodded. No, he said.

Aura slapped him again.

Stop that, TNT said. I might start to like it.

Aura laughed. And how old are you?

Eighteen, he told her truthfully.

He met her stare. Every time he looked at her, he wasn't sure what it was, but something inside him ached.

Well, if I were you — Aura began.

Well, you're not me, are you? Thom said to her.

Good thing, she said, countering him quickly. You'd make a bad girl.

What, like you? he said.

You only wish, she replied, turning away from him, looking down the path.

I wish, Thom said. I wish, I wish, I wish.

It sounded like something Tariq or Duke or Ray would say. He kept wondering how far she was willing to take it, where she would allow him to go. But there always seemed to be a line between them. It was impossible to tell where it was; it kept shifting.

He stared down at her lips, watching her eyes flit over his face, nervous, tentative.

Hey, have you got your stuff? she asked, all business.

Yeah, I got it, Thom replied. He tightened the straps of his backpack, feeling the weight of the spray cans inside, their eventual possibilities.

Well, then, let's do it, she ordered.

What? he said.

Come on, TNT, let's do it. Right here, right now.

What? he said again.

He'd been so preoccupied with Aura that he hadn't seen where they were walking. But there was a large wall in front of them. Thom recognized it instantly. He and Driscoll had buffed it a only few days ago.

Before he knew what she was doing, Aura had zipped open her backpack and whipped out a can of spray paint and a paper stencil which read *WE ARE ALL MADE OF STARS.* Thom watched Aura work quickly and artfully, placing the stencil on the wall and shaking the can, passing over it in several solid lines of black paint.

Helplessly, he stared at her silhouette: the broad, strong shoulders; the boyish hips; her long, firm legs; the taut curve of her waist. The birds flying on her arm as she wrote. When she was finished she pulled the stencil away from the wall, and turned around and smiled at Thom.

What do you think? she said.

Beautiful, he replied in a daze, looking at her.

XXXII.

As I biked to the Ridgeway, the sputtering mist of a million sprinklers sparkled in the early morning sunlight. Everywhere else in the city, the drought of the century had desiccated everyone else's lawns. But here, water was abundant and plentiful and free, and the greens were as green as could be. It was the city of Oz: rainbows bursting in endless spectrums, pots of gold everywhere. I wondered how something could be both so beautiful and so obscene.

But the surprising thing was I didn't care. Not really. Not this morning. I was still slightly hung over, dizzy, delirious, happy. Because last night TNT and I wrote, together, all night.

When I arrived at the clubhouse, Queen Mab was sitting in the centre of the dining room, at a long banquet table, alone, drinking tea, staring out into the trees. She looked like a child sitting at the table, dwarfed by the arched, wooden ceilings and the high, wide windows of glass.

Before I entered the room, she called out to me without turning around. I wondered how she knew. I joined her at the table. The white linen surface of the tabletop was flat and smooth and clean. Outside, the sun crept across the lawn in a slow line of bright, white light. Queen Mab turned to me and then asked if I had a good night. I had promised Chef I wouldn't tell Queen Mab about me shadowing TNT. But then again with Queen Mab one never knew. She had powers none of us really understood. Yeah, I said.

Queen Mab studied me carefully.

You've been hanging out with TNT, haven't you?

She said she could see it in my aura. In the glow around me. Pure pink, she said in her demure, childlike voice. Not your usual blue.

Yes, definitely, she said. It's love. Pure as pure can be. But you haven't acted on it yet, she said. You're holding back.

Which is where the red comes in, she said. On your indecision to realize your feelings in your physical body.

Where does she come up with stuff? It will be up to me to decide, apparently. And then my aura, like me, will change completely.

Then she asked me if I knew what day it was today.

I shook my head. No.

I have seen everything, she said.

I sat there, in silence, wondering how she could see what I could never see, what I could never believe.

Finally, she said: This is the day that Story died.

XXXIII.

What the fuck is this, Driscoll said to Thom. In front of them was Aura's black stencil. Thom leaned forward and looked at it.

I believe it says "We are all made of stars," Thom answered.

I know that, Driscoll said angrily. I'm not stupid. I can read. But what the fuck? This shit's on every wall we've been to. It's a fucking epidemic. And stupid. Buff it.

Thom approached the wall with his paint tray and roller, his heart filled with hate for Driscoll. All morning, he had made Thom buff everything in sight, especially the pieces he and Aura had done. The time they had spent together — those brief, short hours — had been exhilarating; intoxicating. Thom couldn't stop thinking about her. And now here he was, covering it up.

It could be the G7, Thom suggested.

That's the second time you've mentioned the G7 in my presence, Driscoll said. What the fuck do you know about them?

Why don't you tell me, Thom answered boldly. You're the writer.

Driscoll turned around and looked at Thom, bewildered. What? Who the fuck told you that?

Does it matter? Thom retorted.

Driscoll reached out and grabbed Thom by the front of his coveralls, and pulled him sharply into his face.

Listen, I don't know what you think you know, Driscoll

muttered under his breath, but what I do know is that I can make your life a living hell. Do you understand?

Thom's heart flapped with black fear. Driscoll's breath was hot and sharp with the stink of booze. Now he realized what Driscoll had been drinking out of his stainless water canteen. He stared violently into Thom's face, then released his grip and pushed him back against the wall.

Thom stared at Driscoll. You're Everest, aren't you?

Driscoll stared at Thom in silent rage.

Not anymore, he said.

Thom found Driscoll sitting in the driver's seat sipping from his stainless steel canteen, staring out into the park, listening to Led Zeppelin's "No Quarter" at full volume. The truck vibrated with every note. Thom pulled himself up into the passenger seat and sat beside Driscoll.

I haven't been called that name in a long time, Driscoll reflected.

Driscoll glanced sideways and passed Thom the canteen. Raising the wide silver spout to his lips, Thom took a long drink. He was still shaking from when Driscoll had grabbed him. He shuddered as the booze hit him. The music went on in a slow psychedelic frenzy.

What is this?

Scotch, Driscoll said. And water. Well, some water.

You mean to tell me this is what you drink all day? No wonder you're such an asshole.

Driscoll laughed in a sad, self-mocking kind of way.

Yeah, this guy at the Ryder told me who you were. Said you were all city. Back in the day. Thom paused. And a Ryder, too.

Thom passed the canteen back to Driscoll.

Was Winston there at that time too? Thom asked.

Driscoll laughed bitterly. Has there ever been a time when Winston *hasn't* been there? He's the fucking institution, Driscoll said, not the Ryder.

Thom couldn't imagine how hard it was for Driscoll to still be under Winston's supervision. Moving mountains stone by stone and all that bullshit. And here was Driscoll — a.k.a. Everest — being forced to buff every other writer in the city. Thom wondered for the first time if any of his burners were still up.

It must be hard working for him, Thom said.

I don't have a choice, Driscoll said bitterly. I have to. That's what my "contract" says.

Driscoll took a long drink.

You know, they put these writers together at the Ryder — these kids — Driscoll continued, thinking they're going to fix them, like they're going to make everything better, as if all the hurt's going to go away and they're going to go back to their families, their normal lives. But the truth is the other guys you meet at the Ryder end up becoming your family. And nothing is ever normal again.

Thom thought of Tariq, Duke, Ray. Carlos. Omar. Jeremy. Driscoll was right, of course. Even though he barely knew them, Thom felt closer to them than almost anybody.

Did you know any of the G7? Thom asked.

I knew Chef BS when he was at the Ryder, Driscoll said. He was just another writer then, struggling to get up.

Thom tried to keep his cool, but his mind leapt with each new piece of information. Why hadn't Winston said that the G7 had stayed at the Ryder?

Climbing mountains was nothing, Driscoll went on. We *were* mountains. All of us. At least for a little while.

Did you know Story? Thom asked.

Driscoll cleared his throat and took another long drink.

No, Driscoll said. Why, what have you heard about her?

Only what I heard back at the Ryder, Thom replied. How she died trying to catch out. And, you know, other stuff. Rumours, mainly.

Yeah, I've heard that too. Driscoll paused. What else did you hear?

Just something about a Kalpa Path and a Tiger Mountain, Thom surrendered quietly, bowing his head. He turned and looked Driscoll in the eye. And this thing called The Ten. Do you know anything about it?

Driscoll stared hard at Thom.

You may think you know about me. The Ryder. The G7. But that's different. Driscoll looked away. That's something you'll never know. That no one knows.

As they drove back to the Ryder, Thom said nothing more to Driscoll, who sat awash in the music's pounding drone and thunder. Whatever moment of confidence he had dared to share was over. Thom sat silent in the passenger seat, staring out the window, watching the city blur past.

New graff had sprung up everywhere, as if overnight a new generation of writers had been born. Thom saw tags and burners he had never seen before. On mailboxes. Walls. Storefront windows. He and Driscoll had been here only a few days before. For all the buffing they had done, for all the hours he and the other guys from the Ryder had put in, Thom was shocked to see how much more there was. At one time he would have felt smug and happy about it. Now he knew it was just more work he would have to do.

He couldn't wait to see Aura again. Last night he had forgotten about everything else: all the bullshit of everything he was and what he was supposed to do. He felt free. Happy. Like he could do anything.

Outside, on the sidewalk, in the streets, the empty heat stultified everything. Trees seemed to melt, smears of green. As they pulled up to the back entrance of the Ryder, Thom's head was pounding from the jolts of scotch he had shared with Driscoll earlier.

When the truck stopped, Thom moved to open the door, but Driscoll laid his arm across his chest, pinning him to the seat.

What happened today never happened. You never asked me questions; I never answered any. We never talked about anything. Do you understand?

Thom nodded, his heart pounding.

Now get out, Driscoll said.

In his room, Thom lay down and closed his eyes, but he couldn't relax. His mind whirled between what he knew was the truth and what wasn't. It wasn't even that there were lies about the G7, or Story, or Driscoll — there was just an abundance of uncertainty. Thom wasn't so sure anymore — of anything. Including whom he should be loyal to. What did he really owe O'Brien? Chef and the G7 had made him feel more welcome in one night than he ever had.

Thom sat up and moved toward the window, looking out over the river. The couch was still there. As he averted his stare away from the glare of late afternoon sun bouncing off the water, he saw the copy of Blake's collected poems he had taken from Winston's bookshelf.

He picked the book up and stared at the cover again. There was no doubt it was the same tiger stencil he had seen with Driscoll. Thom opened the book and looked inside. None of the pages were marked, except for the front, which was stamped with *Property of Riverside Youth Detention and Rehabilitation Centre. Do Not Remove.*

The coincidence between the stencil and the book was the weirdest thing. And so was the fact that both Winston and Chef had libraries. Then Thom wondered if the G7 had a copy of this book and if he could somehow get access to the Library at the End of the Universe. Maybe Aura could get him in. Thom skimmed through the book, admiring its antiquity, though the taint of erosion and decay drifted up from its worn, browning pages.

There was a knock on his door. Thom looked back. It was Jeremy.

Dude, Winston wants to see you, man, Jeremy said.

Thom frowned at Jeremy. What about?

Dunno. He didn't say. Only that he wants you to come to his office. Right away.

Thom stood on the other side of Winston's door and knocked. The door quickly opened. Inside, Winston was sitting at his desk, talking on the telephone.

You wanted to see me?

Winston nodded silently at him and motioned with his hand for Thom to come in.

Uh-huh. Yeah, well, he's right here now. Uh-huh. Winston looked down at his desk, speaking into the receiver. Of course. You have my guarantee.

Thom looked confusedly at Winston. What was going on? Winston stood up and handed the receiver to him.

It's O'Brien. He wants to talk to you. In private. Winston moved brusquely aside Thom. I'll be back, he warned.

When Winston was gone, Thom brought the receiver to his ear.

Hello?

Is Winston still there?

Thom remembered how much he disliked old-school cops like O'Brien. No, he answered.

O'Brien coughed on the other end of the line. Good. Now tell me what's going on.

Well, you know, Thom said nervously. Commserv with Captain D during the day. Crewing with the G7 at night. He paused. Though I've been working with another writer.

Who's that?

Thom hesitated to say her name, but knew he had to. Aura, he replied.

Yeah, we know about her, O'Brien said impatiently. What else have you learned?

That Chef BS used to be a Ryder.

Good. Is the G7 planning to do something soon?

I don't know, Thom answered. I haven't been privy to any of those conversations.

Why not? You need to be.

Thom could feel O'Brien's impatience over the dead space through the telephone.

I know, Thom answered. But I need to earn their trust.

Do you think they suspect you?

Thom thought about it, remembering the night at the Bridge and then his later time at Io. No, Thom answered. But I have to be careful.

Understood. Anything else you want to tell me?

Yeah, Thom answered. There's this one other thing I keep hearing about.

What's that?

This place called Tiger Mountain. And the Kalpa Path. The Ten. And some writer named Story.

He heard O'Brien take a deep breath. Then, after a pause, he said, What have you heard?

Thom stared at a photograph of two men standing on a snowy peak. In the picture, both of them were wearing goggles, though only one was smiling.

That she was a writer. And a member of the G7. That she died trying to jump a train — do you know anything about her? Or where this Ten is?

O'Brien coughed again. Did you ask Winston about it?

He said it was nothing but a story. Is that true? Do you know anything about it?

O'Brien answered with nothing but silence.

Then finally he said, Do you remember what I first told you? I want real information. Names, addresses. Not ghosts. O'Brien paused. I can't say when I'll call again, but only that I will. Keep up the good work.

And with that, O'Brien hung up.

XXXVI.

I had to find The Ten. I couldn't wait anymore. Someone else had to know something.

I didn't know if The DC knew anything, or if he was going to dish out any intel to me about Story or The Ten, considering Our History and All of That, Et cetera, Et cetera. But I had to ask him.

I went right into the kitchen to look for The DC. Hardcore death metal roared from the small stereo. Lucky for me, DJ O'dysseus was nowhere to be seen. But The DC wasn't behind the line, either. I walked out the back kitchen door and found him outside, leaning against the wall, alone, having a smoke. When he saw me he pulled a long drag from the cigarette and exhaled slowly.

The lovely Aura, The DC crooned flirtatiously. To what do I owe this most honoured pleasure? I stared into his face, despite myself, drawn in by his charm and good looks. I felt the colour rush to my cheeks, my knees weakening.

It was true The DC was good-looking. Killer, in fact. He was just one of those naturally beautiful people, blessed with good genetics and great bone structure. Even when he was a kid, he was beautiful, with black hair and big dark eyes. He'd shown me a picture of himself, once, when he was little, like that. The eyes staring back out of the photograph. Totally confident. Arrogant. Prescient. And totally wary of the future of privilege he would enjoy. Both of The DC's parents were CEOs: Corrupt and Eager for Oppression. In recruiting him for the G7, Chef BS had found a kind of prodigal son in The DC. Someone who he was and could never be, I guess.

The DC flicked the butt of his cigarette into the parking lot. Then he asked me where I had been. How he hadn't seen me in ages. How he missed me. Then our eyes met, and I saw all his arrogance melt away.

You never talk to me anymore, Aura, he said. Now that you're going out every night with TNT.

I decided to ignore him. What did he know about The Ten?

The DC shook his head with laughter. Then he looked down at his feet and shifted side to side. Looked up again. Paused carefully. Smiled. Said it was one of those things. Legendary.

But had he ever seen them, I asked.

He pushed himself off the wall and stood inches from me. What are you after, Aura?

Then I told him I had to find them. I needed to know if they were real. And that I wanted to know where the Kalpa Path started. And that all I wanted was one clue. Just one. I flattered him by saying if there was a piece of graff on a wall somewhere, The DC knew where it would be. And that if anyone knew where the Kalpa Path would start, it would be him.

There was an excruciating silence. And then finally, bitterly, he said to me, Why should I tell you, now?

So I told him it was because of what Mab had told me; it was the anniversary of Story's death. And I wanted to find them; bring The Ten back. Wasn't he even just a little bit intrigued to know if they really existed?

Ever since I started writing, that's all I've ever heard about! The Ten. But I've never *seen* them. I mean, what's so secret about a bunch of writing on a hill?

The DC looked at me with a curious smile and asked me if that's what I thought it was.

You tell me, I replied.

The DC laughed. Then took a step closer to me. Said I was a real piece of work. But that there was a reason it was a secret.

At this point, he was so close to me I could smell his breath, but I didn't dare move.

Oh, really? I said, staring boldly into his eyes. Why's that? The DC angled his head and leaned forward to kiss me, but I backed away. The DC's face twisted into a mask of scorn, hinged with anger and disappointment.

So meddling little toys like you don't mess with it, that's why.

The DC turned his back to me and stormed into the kitchen, slamming the outer door behind him. I followed him and stood at the end of the counter. Asking him to give me just one clue. That I just needed somewhere to start. And then I would leave him alone.

The DC looked up at me, frowning. Told me no. Go away. I was bothering him. I watched as he unsheathed a large chef's knife from a knife block and reached for an onion from the counter behind him.

That'll make you cry, you know, I said.

Nothing makes me cry, The DC shot back at me. I watched as he wedged the stainless steel blade through the centre of the onion, slicing it in half. Nothing, he repeated.

You know, I thought I found the Kalpa Path once, I said to him, lying. One of the first times I ever went out tagging. It was by the river, near this overpass. I didn't know what it was at the time. I went back to look for it a couple of times, but I never could find it again. I could never figure out if it had gotten buffed or tagged over, or if I was in the right place.

Then The DC asked indifferently where it was. I watched him as he cross-sectioned the onion and diced it.

The truth was I knew nothing. But I had to try. So I said it was by the Lombardo Bridge, where Chef had first found me, come to save me from the wasteland of my youth. The DC stopped chopping and asked me if I was sure about that. Yeah, I said.

The DC slowly put his knife down and looked up at me, his dark eyes shining with tears. We held each other's gaze for a few seconds. I watched as The DC raised the bottom of his apron to his face, dabbing his eyes.

I thought nothing made you cry, I said.

I lied, he said. He paused. I thought you didn't know where the Kalpa Path was.

I lied, I said as he smiled back.

XXXVII.

As he approached the park bench — same time, same place — Thom could see Aura in the distance, waiting for him, sitting under the light. As soon as he saw her, Thom felt alert, awake. As if he'd slept a thousand years. She turned her face toward him and smiled. His breath quickened. Tonight, he knew, something would happen. He just didn't know what.

He walked toward her and stopped just before the light, standing outside it.

Hey, she said.

Hey, he replied.

Thom wanted to memorize the way she looked, sitting there, her hair silver and bright, her bare arms exposed to the drift and snare of the hot summer air, the tight fit of her black tank top like one long undulating line.

What? she said, looking at him coyly, laughing, embarrassed-like. What is it? Why are you staring at me like that?

Thom closed his eyes and laughed, shaking his head. Nothing.

What? she urged. Flirting with him so bad it made his stomach churn. What's the matter?

He stepped closer. What could he say? That there was nothing the matter? That what he really wanted was to tell her how beautiful he thought she was? How he had done nothing else but think of her all day? That, in fact, all he wanted was her, more than anything. To kiss her. Pull her down into the grass and put his hands on her. Right now.

But he said nothing.

Her eyes searched him, imploring, as if she were waiting for him to say something more. When he didn't, she turned around and pulled a paint marker out of her backpack and began writing on the back of the bench.

Then, suddenly, red lights flashed. All around them.

Instantly, both of them grabbed their gear and ran toward the trees, throwing themselves down on the ground under a dense line of cedars. Aura lay beside Thom, her breathing spiked with panic. They didn't say anything. Then, two police officers, dressed in uniform, walked toward the bench where he and Aura had been sitting. Thom saw one of the officers switch on a flashlight, sweeping the light around the bench, toward the trees. Thom threw his head down and buried his hands.

Shit. Shit. Shit. Thom cursed in his head to himself silently. *Please. Go. Away. Now.*

If they were caught, they were carrying all the evidence with them. And even though he knew he was protected by O'Brien, if he was not charged, Aura and the rest of the G7 would know something funny was up and his cover would be blown. Either way, he was screwed.

A minute passed. Then another, and another. Eventually the voices of the officers stopped. Thom looked up. They were gone. He looked slowly left, then right. There was no sign of them. He looked at Aura, her eyes wide.

Do you think they saw us? she whispered excitedly.

Maybe, Thom replied.

Fuuuck, Aura sighed as she rolled over on her back and breathed deeply, that was *amazing*.

Thrill-seeker, huh? Thom said with a derisive smile. You are seriously messed up, you know that? Freak.

Aura laughed again.

Thom watched her chest rise and fall with laughter. She was breathing hard, stealing short little jabs of air. He studied the curve of her neck, following it down to her chest.

What should we do now? Aura said to him, her voice a whisper.

He fought the urge to kiss her.

I don't know, Thom replied, turning his head away. But we've got to get out of here.

Wait, she said to Thom with a calm, steady voice. Her eyes shone at him in the darkness. I know a place we can go.

As they stepped toward the edge of the river in the darkness, their headlamps on, Thom wondered if Aura really knew where she was going.

They had been walking for more than an hour: up and down side streets, through empty industrial neighbourhoods, winding their way along a path beside the river, toward some bridge. Wherever they were, Thom recognized none of it from his outings with Driscoll.

Are you sure this is the right way? he asked doubtfully.

Oh, this is it, Aura said. It should be right here, somewhere.

Where are we? Thom asked.

Deep in the heart of darkness, Aura said. Of suburbia, that is.

You know this neighbourhood?

Damn right, Aura said. One of the first pieces I ever did was out here. Once you get away from the river, it's nothing but McMansions, as far as the eye can see. Urban sprawl, like a cancer, taking over everything. She paused. Maybe it's still here ...

Thom scanned the underside of concrete above him. What am I looking for, exactly?

Whether she didn't hear him or was ignoring him, Aura didn't answer Thom as they walked under the bridge.

Did you grow up around here? he asked.

Aura looked at him suspiciously. Where, here? Nah. My hood's over there, beyond those trees —

In the valley of the newlywed and nearly dead?

Aura laughed lightly. Yeah, something like that. Where do you live?

Thom knew he was being tested, interrogated, tried.

I dunno. In some neighbourhood, Thom lied. I don't even know what it's called, other than that it sounds like some insane asylum. Richmond Hill Valley Acre Farms. It's my dad's house. All I know is that all the houses look the same and all the people who live inside them look the same.

Aura smiled, charmed.

I know, she went on, all these people with their big houses and their 2.2 kids and their SUVs and their big screen TVs and their La-Z-Boys — the truth is, they're just clones. Zombies to the consumerist system that feeds them. Graff's the only "real thing" out here.

Thom watched Aura's headlamp flicker along the wall. He remembered when he had felt the same way. Frustrated, forgotten. Wanting to change the way he saw the landscape around him to reflect how he felt, what he thought, what he wanted to see. To be heard, to be seen. To piss people off. Yes, to scream, to rage: *wake up*.

It's still here, he heard Aura say. Right here.

Thom looked where Aura was pointing. There, on the wall, Thom read a single phrase in black letters: *STOP WASTING YOUR LIFE TO MAKE ENDS MEET TO GO HOME AT NIGHT TO YOUR COLOUR TV.*

He looked at Aura. Yours?

She nodded. No. I stole it. From SAMO. You know, Jean-Michel Basquiat? He was a graffiti artist first, you know.

Thom thought of Driscoll. Yeah, I know.

He scanned his headlamp over the letters, admiring their size, the grade of line.

Do you keep a sketchbook for your ideas? he asked.

Yeah, she replied. I always have. My black book, I call it. You?

Nah, Thom said. My sketches seem to lose something when they're not on a wall, not out in public, you know?

I've heard other writers say that, Aura said. But it's a good place to try stuff out. New phrases, writing styles. Not every idea is a good one. It's important to work something through. Chef told me that.

I wish I could, Thom confessed.

What? You can't draw? Aura teased.

Yeah, my hand freezes up. I can do burners and throw-ups all night long, but draw? Nah.

Aura studied her piece in the glare of her headlamp. Moths and insects flickered toward the light.

I'm surprised it's still here, Aura said. I thought for sure the Graffpol would have buffed it by now.

No, they usually don't get out this far, Thom said.

Aura turned her headlamp toward Thom. He felt his face burn under the hot glare of Aura's bright light, her eyes shrouded with suspicion. How would you know? she asked.

Now it was Thom's turn to ignore her.

Then, suddenly, he saw something, behind Aura's head. What is that?

Aura turned around and followed the direction of his headlamp. There, small and white, was a single letter *K*, edged in a corner under the bridge.

This must be it, Aura said in a whisper, the start of the Kalpa Path.

Thom couldn't believe what he just heard. *This* is the Kalpa Path? he exclaimed.

She stared at him, incredulous. You know about it? she asked. And Tiger Mountain, too?

It's all I've heard about since I've been here, Thom said with excitement, not caring he was probably giving himself away.

Do you know where The Ten are? she asked.

No. Do you?

No, Aura said disappointedly. I guess that just means we can look for it together, now.

Thom focused his headlamp on the single letter, while Aura stared at it in a kind of awed silence.

I never believed it was real, Aura finally said. Not until now.

But how, Thom asked, looking around, how is this the start?

The letters, Aura said. Obviously they must follow in order. Starting from here. Once we find them all, the last one will lead us to Tiger Mountain where The Ten must be!

Thom quickly scanned the area around the K with his headlamp. So, uh, what kind of clue are we looking for to find the next letter?

That, Aura answered, is what I don't know.

Thom stared at the underside of concrete.

There's nothing here, Thom said.

Keep looking, Aura urged, there has to be something.

Where are we again? Thom asked.

Kyle Parkway, Aura replied. Why?

Thom looked at Aura. Think about it, he said. *Kalpa Path, Kyle Parkway —*

Aura swung around and bathed Thom in a pool of light. I get it, she said. They both start with *K*! That means that the letters *correspond*. So, since this is *K*, and the next letter is *A*, that must mean that the next letter must be somewhere near a location with the letter *A*. Thom noted the excitement in her voice. So. If the path follows the river, then the next location should be Adelaide Street, to the east.

Aura flashed Thom a smile, her eyes bright. TNT, you are a fucking genius!

Thom looked down with a smile and shrugged involuntarily, casting off her compliment. But inside he was burning with anticipation. He could hardly wait to see where Aura would lead him next, where the Kalpa Path ended up, and what The Ten might be.

C'mon, Aura called out. Let's go.

Thom stepped off into the darkness and followed her, staring ahead at the small circle of light from her headlamp as she weaved along the trail of the river.

XXXVIII.

We found it. Last night. Me and TNT. Fucking beautiful genius he is, letter by letter. The Kalpa Path. What we figured out — well, what he did, anyway — was that the letters in Kalpa Path corresponded to actual locations. Unfortunately we didn't finish all the letters last night. But we will. Soon. Maybe tonight.

I can't believe he's been looking for The Ten, too. I know we're going to find it, together. Just like in my dream.

It was a real kick to find each letter, and once we knew what we were looking for, everything seemed to fall together. TNT got right into it. Somehow I thought it would be more complicated, but the letters were all along the river. I finally figured out why I hadn't seen them before: because even though they're easy to see, they're unusually placed. They're not near any other writing. They're in hard-to-reach, out-of-the-way places. What's even more miraculous is that none of them have been buffed. Not a single one. But I'm happy they haven't. The letters, in their singularity, have this otherworldly presence. They stand alone, symbols of something greater, a secret pointing to something much larger.

Now we just have to go back. Another night. Together. Me and TNT.

Working beside him all night was exquisite torture. Hearing the sound of his voice speaking to me in the darkness as we

walked along the river. This ever-present tension between us;
the energy between our bodies electric. Just one look from him
sent sparks flying, like fireworks shooting off from between
my thighs. The great hotness of the night all around us. Desire
a whip I flayed myself with: wishing and wishing I had never ever
promised anything to Chef BS.

I felt like I was going to crack. Watching TNT. O my tempta-
tion. To take him, to feel him move against me. Everything, I say.

Everything. About. Him. Turns. Me. On.

I want to tell Chef that I can't work with TNT anymore. But I
will not do that.

I will smile, smile, smile and lie, lie, lie.

Why? Because there's a job that needs to be done that I said
I would do and there's work that's been done already, and I
can't help it if I believe that the work of the G7 is a cause that is
greater than any of us.

So I will keep going out at night with TNT, accepting of what
I promised Chef. I can hide my love for TNT in a million different
ways, in so many places, no one will ever know or even suspect
that it's there. Even just the slightest look I can hide away. Place
in a pocket of sky. Throw behind a star.

Only I will know where all the love will go.

On the edge. Of the ledge. Overlooking the chasm below.

Birds fly. I cry. Give me wings to grow.

XXXIX.

Yo, brother, wake up.

Thom feels an arm on his shoulder, firmly shaking him. He
opens his eyes slowly, staring into the smiling brown eyes of
Duke, who is leaning over his bed.

Wakey-wakey, Duke says. It's rise and shine time at the Ryder.

Thom was dreaming about a train. A black car, rattling on the tracks. Going through mountains.

No no no, don't close your eyes. Yo, you got to wake up, Duke says, more urgently. Winston's orders. Duke's voice is faraway, fuzzy, in another time and place.

In the dream, someone else was with him. *Who was it?*

Duke jabs Thom gently in the shoulder again.

What did you get into last night, brother? You're still wearing your damn clothes.

Then Thom remembers. It was Aura.

You got to get up, Thom hears Duke say. Or else I'm going to get Tariq and Ray in here. They gonna mess you up, man. And you won't like it. Especially Tariq. He's got some mean breath in the morning, I tell you. You ain't gonna like it.

Thom feels his only hour of sleep like an anchor weighting him to the bed. He can't lift an arm, a leg. Gravity holds him down, like he's being buried. What were he and Aura doing in his dream? Then he remembers: they were in a room in a house, her lips kissing his, light in her mouth. And birds, birds flying. His eyelids flutter open. He looks blankly at Duke.

That's it, my man, Duke says. See? I knew if I told you Tariq and Ray was coming, you were gonna wake up.

What time is it? Thom says groggily.

Time for you to get up, Duke replies. Driscoll's waiting outside on your ass cuz you got Graffpol duty today. And he don't look too happy, neither.

What? Thom groans as he pulls himself upright. Every muscle in his body aches, as if his dream was real. Then he realizes Duke was right. He looks down: he fell asleep wearing his clothes. Duke throws him his coveralls.

Good thing you're already dressed. Captain D doesn't like to wait.

Outside, Thom staggered to the truck, trying to wake up.

Where the hell have you been? Driscoll said as Thom opened the door and sat down in the passenger seat. You look like shit. Again.

Thom shuddered convulsively, then reached forward and turned off the air conditioning.

It's fucking cold, Thom said.

A lot fucking colder than it's going to be if you don't turn that a/c back on, right fucking now, Driscoll barked.

His words dug like a blade. Thom turned away in silence. After what happened the last time they were together, he didn't want to give rise to Driscoll's anger again.

Now don't be like that, Driscoll said to him, noting his sullenness. Just because I nearly beat the shit out of you last time doesn't mean we can't work together as friends today.

The word "friends" bristled in the air of the truck cab. As if, Thom thought to himself with bitterness. If he was a mountain once, he was nothing now. Winston was right. Whatever was left of the writer in him couldn't be trusted. And that was the bottom line.

Later that morning, Driscoll drove through a part of the city Thom had never seen. They rolled through exclusive neighbourhoods, driving past gated driveways. *No Trespassing* signs were everywhere. Finally, Driscoll parked the truck on the side of the road. Through a black wrought iron fence, Thom overlooked a golf course and its dazzling green lawn.

What the fuck are we doing here? Thom sighed. There's no graff here. And if there is, I don't give a shit about it. They can hire some private removal company. I'm tired. I want to go back to the Ryder.

Driscoll stared at Thom as if he hadn't heard a word he'd said.

I want to show you something, Driscoll said. Something you might find interesting. Follow me.

Thom and Driscoll walked along the fence line of a golf course. At one point, Thom was pretty sure they were trespassing, since the wrought iron fence disappeared and there was just endless green space. In the distance Thom saw pale figures standing on the grass, leaning and twisting against the perfect blue sky. He heard a far-off *thwack*. In front of him, Driscoll pressed on, into a line of trees.

Where the fuck are we going? Thom yelled at O'Brien. His voice seemed to get swallowed up in the trees that towered over them, in their shafts of broken sunlight.

Driscoll stopped and took a drink and offered his canteen to Thom, who refused.

Go on, Driscoll said. You can't hate me forever.

Thom stared at Driscoll. Yeah, I can.

Driscoll laughed, drinking. You wouldn't be the first.

Panic flared hot in Thom's throat, like he couldn't breathe. What was Driscoll up to?

Can you please tell me where the fuck we're going?

Driscoll's face widened in a dark smile. We're almost there.

Where?

Driscoll swung around and waved his hand through the air with an exaggerated, dramatic flourish, pointing to the trees.

There, he said.

Thom was getting tired of Driscoll's games. I'm going back to the truck, Thom said. You know what? Fuck that. I'm going back to the Ryder.

Thom turned around and started walking. Then he heard Driscoll's voice, clear and calm, yell out at him:

I thought you wanted to see Tiger Mountain.

Thom spun around and looked at Driscoll in confusion. Just when Thom thought he knew who he was, he had to pull something like this. Captain D was a total paradox.

Face it. You need me. Whether you like it or not, Driscoll said. He offered Thom his stainless steel canteen.

Who was the real Driscoll? Thom wasn't sure.

Reluctantly, Thom reached forward and took the canteen from his hand and drank.

XL.

Got another message from Chef through Mab today. To meet him at the Library. As soon as I could get there. As I climbed the stairs, I remembered the first time I had been brought to the Library at the End of the Universe, shortly after I'd joined the G7. Chef had built the library himself, carefully selecting a collection of books in history, poetry, anthropology, philosophy, and art. He truly believed that one day books as physical objects would become obsolete, and he wanted the G7 to have a place where we could all come and read, without, as he called it, a "mediated" approach. Reading, he believed, should take place in the body, not in the mind. He wanted to create a space without computers, without screens. A restful space for rumination, meditation. For dreams.

As I entered the Library, I found Chef sitting in his favourite dilapidated chair by the window. As I approached him, he looked up at me and smiled. I asked him what he was reading.

Chef held up the book's cover for me to see. *The Space of Literature* by Maurice Blanchot.

Interesting? I asked as I pulled up a chair beside him.

Very, he replied. He pulled out a package of clove cigarettes and offered me one. I declined, watching as he slowly lit one with a packet of wooden matches. I watched his fine, delicate fingers strike the side of the box and light the dark cigarette. Sweet, heady smoke blew around him.

Then he asked me how my mission was coming with TNT. Fine, I replied. Fine. Hoping Mab hadn't told him anything. Which I knew was impossible. But still, I could hope. Couldn't I?

Chef took a long, thoughtful drag on his cigarette and asked me if TNT had told me anything unusual about himself, or if there was anything he needed to know about him.

No, not really.

Oh, Chef said with dark interest. Where does he live?

Oh, you know, I said lightly, just some suburban neighbourhood.

Chef exhaled and asked me if it was Mr. Rogers's neighbourhood. I said I didn't understand, and Chef looked at me and smiled this crazy strange smile and asked me if I'd been there. So of course I answered no. Then Chef held my gaze with a calculating, piercing stare and asked me: Do you think he's a rat?

Silence filled the Library. Chef took another drag from his cigarette and stubbed it out in a vintage ashtray. Up close, I was struck by how distorted his face has become accommodating his missing eye: the nerves and muscles around his face contorted by the vacant, expressionless socket.

No — I replied, shocked. How could Chef make such an accusation? And with what proof?

Then Chef asked if I had ever gone home with him. No, I answered, offended. I told him I wasn't breaking The Rule this time.

Chef's body stiffened. I know that, Aura, his voice rising, but have you seen him go home, after you've been out together?

I remembered what Mab had once told me about how Chef

had lost his eye. Apparently, when he was younger, he had a lazy eye which he got teased about relentlessly. He got into a fist fight in grade school, and had been punched so badly that it permanently damaged the eye and all the tissue around it. Eventually, it became so unstable it had to be removed permanently. He didn't go back to school that year.

I forced myself to remember the times I had been with TNT. The questions that went unanswered. I had been so focused on learning about Story, the Kalpa Path, discovering Tiger Mountain ... My stomach knotted. Could I have been so easily distracted from the truth right in front of me?

No, I said to Chef, ashamed.

Don't you think that's important, Aura? To know who he is? Everyone else in the G7 gets shadowed before they're accepted into the crew. Or are you willing to jeopardize the entire mission and goals of the G7 because you haven't taken the time to do what I have asked you to do?

Chef didn't even wait for me to answer. He rose from the chair and stood in the sunlight by the window, looking down into the street. He sighed deeply.

I'm disappointed, he said. I trusted you.

His words stung me. I had failed him.

Please, I pleaded.

And then Chef told me that ever since Story died, the police had been looking for a way to connect him to her death. They believed he must have been responsible somehow, even though he was nowhere near her when she died. But they needed someone to blame, to catch.

He was no longer a minor, he said. If he were to be caught, he could not be protected. There would be no juvie for him. No commserv, no rehabilitation. He would be tried in court, as an adult. Defenceless against whatever sentence they levelled against him. He needed protection. He needed me to find out who TNT really was.

It wasn't even the prospect of getting caught that really scared him, he said. Don't you see? It's what will happen to the G7. If they destroy us, if we let them, they will burn down everything we've created, destroy everything we've built. They will erase our resistance. Make us irrelevant. As if we never even happened. They will buff us out of existence. Then they will seize control; dictate the public imagination. And then, he concluded breathlessly, they will win.

XLI.

Thom and Driscoll walked through the trees. The city seemed miles away. Even the world of O'Brien and Winston, the Ryder, the G7 — all of it — seemed intangible, impossible even, belonging to another time and place, another reality. Thom didn't get it. Why was Driscoll showing him this now? It didn't make sense. And if they really were near Tiger Mountain, it was nowhere near where he and Aura had been looking last night when they'd stopped their search downtown. Nor was it anywhere near the tiger stencil he had first seen.

Driscoll stopped. Do you hear that? he whispered to Thom.

Thom pretended to listen to whatever he was supposed to be listening for but heard nothing.

The train, Driscoll said. Do you hear it? It's on the other side of the forest. He paused. On the other side of the mountain.

Thom listened again. This time he heard it: an interminable loop of sound. Distant and clattering; screeching on rails.

Did you like being a hopper? Driscoll asked.

Yeah, Thom lied, searching the inside of his brain for things to say that he'd only heard from other writers. It's pretty sick.

You get to see the country from the inside of a moving train. Plus you meet some totally cool people along the way.

Driscoll studied Thom's reaction carefully. Yeah, I'd like to try it one day.

Then he heard another sound: a faint rushing.

Thom followed Driscoll's gaze through the trees. What's that? he asked.

What do you think? Driscoll said. The river.

They walked to the riverbank. At its edge, Driscoll removed his sunglasses and pulled his shirt off and bent down on his hands and knees and ran a handful of cool water over his head, splashing himself. Thom stared at the strength of Driscoll's arms and shoulders, his solid torso. He was pure muscle, hard and lean as a rope. There was a reason he had been named Everest.

Where is Tiger Mountain? Thom asked impatiently. I don't see it.

It's right there, Driscoll said, pointing his arm across the river, into the trees. Just there. Straight ahead. See?

Thom looked. There was nothing. Nothing but trees. Nothing else.

I don't see it, Thom repeated. This time his voice was more urgent, desperate. I thought you said it was here.

Oh, you can't *see* it, Driscoll said, standing up. Not in the way that you think you might see a mountain, you know, from a distance. But it's there. Hidden inside the forest. You can just see the tip of it, right there.

Thom looked again. Then, almost imperceptibly, he saw a point of what looked like the top of a house.

Thom couldn't believe what he was looking at. It was a roof peak.

But that's not a *mountain* — Thom blurted out. Even saying the words out loud didn't make sense to him. And besides, it was nowhere near where he had been told. He thought of the excitement he and Aura had shared last night along the Kalpa Path, finding the letters. He looked at the white triangle of the roof peak, floating there, in the middle of the trees.

If it's not a mountain why is it called Tiger Mountain?

Driscoll put his shirt and sunglasses back on.

Because, Driscoll answered slowly, when the sun sets, it turns orange and the shadows of the trees turn into stripes and it looks like it's on fire. And when the wind blows, it moves, like a tiger moves, but stays still as a mountain.

Thom was speechless. He'd never heard Driscoll talk like that before.

Anything can be a mountain, Driscoll said. It's only a matter of perspective.

But how —

Because I know this city better than anyone. I've seen all of its cracks, its holes, its brokenness — all exposed in the bright light of day. And I've known all the writers that have tried, in their own way, to fill in those spaces, with their words, their art, their music.

So you knew Story?

Driscoll nodded. Yes.

But I thought you said you didn't. Thom was confused.

I lied, Driscoll said.

And what about the Kalpa Path? Thom stammered. Did you lie about that? Or does that exist?

Driscoll smiled slyly.

Which one? There are many Kalpa Paths, but only one true path that leads to Tiger Mountain. The others are just decoys to keep the toys away.

Thom recalled him and Aura last night, chasing correspond-
ing letters they thought would lead them to The Ten. Chasing
ghosts.

Where is it then?

Isn't it obvious? Driscoll asked.

Thom realized, instantly: the river. He looked across the
water and there, directly across from them, was a small opening
in the forest — revealing a narrow path — leading up into the
trees.

Thom studied Driscoll's profile in the sunlight. He was silent.

Well, Driscoll said plainly, I've got to take you back to the
Ryder. Let's go.

What? Thom was stunned. Aren't you going to show me
Tiger Mountain? After bringing me this far?

Driscoll looked at Thom with a tired smile.

Some mountains aren't always made for climbing. Besides,
I have a feeling you'll be coming back.

Driscoll had brought him here knowing he would tell
someone else. Had this been his plan all along? Thom staggered
at the possibility. Had Driscoll been testing him all this time?
To see if he could entrust him this information?

Why me? Why are you showing this to me?

He stared Thom in the eye.

Last time we were out you said things no one's ever said to
me. You reminded me of someone I once knew. Someone I'd
forgotten about.

Thom felt the back of his neck prickle with sweat. Why would
Driscoll trust him now? He looked up at the white triangle in
the trees. Then he turned back to Driscoll, unafraid.

This is a trick, right? You're just showing me this to get
me into trouble with Winston, aren't you? To burn me? I just
know it —

No, Driscoll replied. I've been carrying this secret for a long time. I just needed to share it with someone before I ... Driscoll paused, stuttering on the end of his sentence. I don't know. It just felt like the right thing to do. That's all.

Driscoll paused again, his face changing back to its usual, hard mask.

Now. I have to get your sorry ass back to the Ryder before Winston starts asking questions. Why don't you lead? You'll want to know your way through the trees when it's dark.

XLII.

That night I waited for TNT at the bench by the river, our usual meeting place. I scanned the park, looking for him, trying not to think of why he might be late. Then I saw him: a skinny line running through the darkness toward me. I couldn't stop thinking about everything Chef had said at the Library. About everything I should have done to find out who he was. About everything I didn't do.

One of the things I loved about being in the G7 was that our personal histories began and ended with our activities as a crew. All I ever was when I was with them was Aura, graffiti girl. Me. The me whom I wanted to be. An identity that existed outside all the bullshit of everything I was expected to be by my parents. School. Society. Et cetera. As Aura, I was more persona than actual living body. Which was how I wanted it to be. I could control that, direct how others saw me.

I never asked anything of TNT because I assumed he wanted to protect his anonymity for the same reasons. That was why I never followed him home. I didn't want to expose him in that way. It was wrong.

But Chef was right. We needed to know more.

As he came closer, I steeled myself for what I would say. Did he know how long I'd been waiting? Where the hell had he been? But as he approached, all I could see was the excitement brimming in his face, as if he was about to burst.

Did I have my headlamp, he asked breathlessly.

Of course, I replied. He bent down and zipped open his backpack and threw me a plastic bag and told me to put anything I didn't want to get wet inside.

I couldn't understand what the hell was going on. Are you okay? I asked him. And he laughed and said, fine, fine. Then he asked me if I knew how to swim. And again, I said, yes, of course. Then he said good, like he was checking off some kind of checklist in his mind. Then he said he needed one more thing and I was like, whoa, whoa, whoa. I thought we were going to Tiger Mountain.

And then he said: We are. The *real* Tiger Mountain.

I take it it's not downtown, I said. He shot me this slightly lopsided grin that drove me crazy in the best possible way. I asked him how he had found it, but he said he couldn't say. That someone had told him in secret and that he had promised to keep it that way.

How could he know where The Ten were when he had only just got here, and I had been looking for years? I felt cheated. As if I should have been the one to find out first. It wasn't fair. TNT smiled at me again.

So, do you want to see it or not? he asked.

I nodded.

The only thing left he needed to know was how to get to this golf and country club. The Kalpa Path started around there somewhere. But he didn't know how to get to it. It was called the Ridgeway, he said. My mouth dropped open and I saw the cartoon bubble blossoming impossible, ridiculous over my head as I said the words: *Are you fucking kidding me? No way. I, like, work there. Every. Day.*

At which point TNT said to me, so you know where it is then?

To which I nodded and heard myself saying to him yes, I know, yes, yes, a million times yes.

XLIII.

Thom stared down at the small square patch of light in front of him. In its radius, the forest floor took shape beneath his feet, shifting in colours of green and brown among black shadows. Before the light, he could see every detail of every leaf, every branch, every tree — but outside that, beyond where the light touched, there was nothing but darkness. All he could see was what was right in front of him, what was in his headlamp, his line of vision. It was kind of how he felt about Story and the G7. He knew there were things about them, things he couldn't see that were out there, things that just weren't before the light. Not yet.

As he broke trail along the path Driscoll had shown him, Thom recalled his earlier conversation with O'Brien just before he had left the Ryder to meet Aura.

He had been called to Winston's office again. A fact that didn't go unnoticed by the other Ryders, who thought Thom was getting in shit. Little did they know they weren't far off from the truth.

On the phone, O'Brien was all business, and didn't waste any time in wanting to know what else Thom had heard about Story, Tiger Mountain and The Ten. And who had told him. Thom didn't reveal that he knew the location but said that he had learned more information. He didn't think it would do any harm to mention Driscoll's name, since he thought he would probably know who he was through Winston, but he couldn't have been more wrong.

Driscoll, Thom told him. Captain D. You know, the lead guy of the Graffpol? My crew leader? The asshole I told you about?

At the other end of the line there was nothing but O'Brien's officious silence.

Then O'Brien said: Are you sure his name is Driscoll?

Yeah, Thom answered.

Are you sure? O'Brien asked again.

I just told you it was, Thom said, annoyed.

I meant his *real* name, O'Brien said.

That is his real name, Thom said. Besides, what the fuck does it matter? Thom said to him suddenly, impulsively. He was tired of O'Brien's bullshit. Listen, I've told you everything I know. Besides, I thought it was the G7 you were after, not Driscoll. He's already been caught. He already works for you. Remember what you said? You just wanted names? Addresses? Here's one for you: the Library at the End of the Universe. 401½ Richmond Street, third floor. Southwest corner of Dundas and Richmond Street.

The anger and sarcasm rose in Thom's voice.

That's where they're plotting The Next Big Thing that's never going to fucking happen. Fuck. Why do you even give a shit? Somewhere in this shitty city, right now, while I'm wasting my fucking time talking to you, some girl is getting date raped or some kid's trying coke for the first time, and you want me to give you the skinny on a bunch of no-names with some cans of spray paint?

Thom couldn't stop. It was flowing out of him now: all the hate and resentment he had for O'Brien; for the police; for everything they symbolized.

Graffiti doesn't happen in a void, Thom said. It's a reaction. Against tyranny, hate, oppression. Yes, poverty. Crime. Why don't you catch some real criminals instead of worrying whether or not your stupid city looks pretty? The G7 is the least of your worries. Fuck.

Silence.

Everest, or Driscoll, as you call him, doesn't work for me, O'Brien said quietly. He only works for Winston.

I don't care who he works for. Didn't you listen to what I just said? Thom said. Why don't you tell me the real reason I'm doing this? Because of Story? Well, Story's dead. I don't get why any of this fucking matters, he hissed.

There was more silence, then finally O'Brien spoke. His voice was quiet, apologetic, resigned.

Because Story is my daughter, O'Brien said.

The words hung, electric, between them.

And I need to know the truth about what happened, O'Brien said, his voice breaking.

Thom was stunned. His memory raced back to O'Brien's office. The family pictures behind his desk. He tried to remember details — but at the time all he had seen were empty, smiling faces of strangers who had meant nothing to him.

O'Brien's silence grew on the other end. In its wordlessness, Thom could sense O'Brien's helplessness, his panic, the random nature of his fear. A father's absolute unknowing. His unconditional love. Thom thought of his own father. He wondered: would he have felt that same way, too? His mother? It had been years since he had been away, but they had never stopped looking for him. Sadness surged through him, but he pushed the thought away.

I would appreciate it if you didn't mention this to anyone, especially Winston.

Thom listened to O'Brien's sharp, stifled breathing on the other end of the line.

He couldn't even mumble *I'm sorry* before O'Brien hung up.

Thom turned around to see Aura in the glow of his head-lamp, walking behind him. She had led them to the Ridgeway; now it was his turn to lead them to Tiger Mountain. Thom remembered Driscoll's last words to him: *You'll want to know your way through the trees when it's dark.* Part of him expected there to be nothing on the other side of the river, like it was all a big joke. He could see Driscoll's face now, a spectre floating in front of him, laughing at him. *Just like I first said, asshole, one size fits all.*

But Thom knew Driscoll wasn't lying. Not this time.

Thom could smell the dead heat in the trees. And hear beyond, in the darkness, through the forest, the same train he had heard with Driscoll. As he listened to its long, sad echo, Thom thought about Story.

Whatever had happened to her, O'Brien couldn't touch him anymore. No one could. Not with what he knew now. Thom should have known from the beginning that O'Brien didn't really care about the G7. Now, with what he knew about Story, everything had changed. He was free. But he wasn't going to leave. Not yet. He had a few more things he had to find out. He wasn't going to give up now.

Everywhere his light touched was wild, green: unmasked, revealing the possible truth of things.

XLIV.

At the river's edge, I stood in the darkness, TNT beside me, watching the murky black water churn under the light from our headlamps. As I flashed my light downstream, tree stumps stuck out left and right, like disconnected arms waving from a watery hell. From the middle of the river came a warm green stink, like rotten lettuce. Bodies. Death.

I asked him how this could be the Kalpa Path. But then he showed me the proof, almost indistinguishable in the trees, of a triangle that was supposed to be Tiger Mountain. Or so TNT said.

I looked down at my bare feet, the black mud caked between my toes. I thought of our shoes, tied together with our clothes, in a plastic bag inside his backpack. Wearing only my bra and panties, I felt TNT's light scan over me. I flashed mine back at him. Barefoot, bare-chested, wearing only his boxers, TNT told me to walk in and swim beside him. *Now.*

Do you have to keep that thing pointed at me, I said, checking out his hard, plum-coloured nipples, the bulge in his shorts.

I'm not going to put my head under the water, I said to him. Not in this river. Not with what I've seen.

TNT teased me for being chickenshit, and then I heard it: the unmistakable *swhish-swhish* of his feet as he stepped into the river. I scanned my headlamp toward his direction and watched him disappear into the water, holding up the backpack with one strong, lean arm as he waded across, his head above the surface. I tried not to think about what might be down at the bottom, and turned my headlamp off.

Darkness was everywhere — in the water, in the sky, in the night — all of it sticking to me, clinging onto me, filling up all the holes inside of me. I could hardly breathe. The line of water crept up my legs, splashing up on my inner thighs. Then at my stomach. My neck. The river bottom squishy and cold. My toes felt their way over the edges of slick, slime-covered logs and branches, sharp rocks and stones. I didn't breathe until I was across on the other side. When I got there, I saw the outline of TNT's body on the dark, wet shore. He reached inside his backpack and threw me my stuff. We dressed in the darkness silently.

TNT waited for me at the base of the path that led up into the trees. As I watched the direction of his headlamp flash upward into the dense forest, I realized it was the same path as the one he had shown me in my dream.

Chef was right. I didn't know who TNT was. Maybe I never would. But I trusted him. And maybe for no other reason than because I had dreamed of him and this moment and because he had led me here.

I reached out and slipped my hand into his. It was cool and smooth, just like after a rain. And it occurred to me that maybe all the time I was dreaming about Story, I had really been dreaming of TNT. I just couldn't see him. Maybe he was what Story was telling me to see. He looked at me, his eyes full of wonder, searching mine. I felt dizzy, light, like the ground was going to give out under my feet.

He gripped my hand.

Let's go climb a mountain, he said.

XLV.

Thom wasn't sure exactly what he was supposed to be look-ing for, but he had a feeling that once he saw it, he would instinctively know and a voice would go off, like a shot, telling him *that* is it, *that* is Tiger Mountain.

It was that voice that he listened for as he threaded his way through the trees, looking for the one thing, whatever that was, that would lead him in the right direction. Right now he didn't know if what he found would make any difference to anyone. All he knew was that he was this far in and he wasn't about to back out now. Thom was beginning to think Driscoll was trying to tell him something else. Maybe about Story; or him. Why else would he show him the way? What other secrets had he been carrying? Now that he knew what he knew, he would not be afraid to ask Driscoll, point blank, about anything. Or Winston.

So. What *exactly* do you know about Story? Thom probed Aura as they walked together through the woods. Does anyone know her real name?

No ... no one really knew that much about her other than the work that she did. She lived a secret life she kept hidden from everyone, including Chef.

It was no wonder, Thom thought to himself, if she was O'Brien's daughter.

Maybe it was something she even wanted to hide from herself, he said.

What do you mean?

Beyond the range of his headlamp he could see fireflies, electric green, pulsing on and off. Maybe she didn't even want to know who she was, Thom said cryptically. He paused thoughtfully. So what are The Ten again? he continued.

No one really knows, Aura answered. It's rumoured they're a set of rules. Commandments. A code of some kind.

A code? To what?

I don't know, Aura replied. That's just what I heard.

From who?

Oh, you know. Here and there, over the years. Ever since I became a writer I wanted to find The Ten. Story's the reason I became a writer. The tone of her voice was deep and flat, unironic. I guess I can say now I really am following in her footsteps.

Thom stared into Aura's face. There was an innocence to her, he thought, but an edge, too. Her hand had seemed so strong in his: fierce, restless, unafraid.

And then, out of the corner of his eye, Thom saw something hard and white. Quickly, he swung his light back over it, double checking to see what it was. Because he couldn't believe what he was seeing, right in front of him. It was a house, an old dilapidated cottage, in white clapboard, abandoned, in the trees.

This is it, she said breathlessly. Look.

On the front door was a spray-painted tiger, hovering over a triangle under a sea of flames. On the triangle was a single letter: X. The Roman numeral for ten.

Tyger, tyger, burning bright, in the forests of the night — Thom began, remembering the poem.

What immortal hand or eye dare frame thy fearful symmetry, Aura said, finishing the line.

You know the poem? Thom said.

Of course, Aura said as she brushed against him and moved toward the door. It's Blake. Chef has a copy in the Library.

XLVI.

At first, I was afraid to open the door. I stood before it, my hand in mid-air, hovering over the door handle. The tiger burned in the centre of my gaze. Was it a warning, I wondered, like the entrance to a tomb? My heart pounded with excitement, expectation. And fear.

I had waited so long for this moment.

TNT sidestepped me and turned the handle and the door swung easily into the empty house. Then he motioned for me to go in first.

As I stepped over the threshold, into the front room, the floorboards creaked under my feet. I scanned quickly, left and

right, looking. The walls were undecorated, painted in what had
once been sea green but had now faded. Water stains bled down
the walls from the ceiling. Huge swags of cobwebs drifted in their
corners, guileless. Dust and dirt were everywhere. In the corner,
I saw a pile of scat: I was not the only other animal to have
been here. In the dank, hot heat, the house smelled rancid, like
piss and death.

I swung around, realizing TNT was no longer behind me. I
said his name, waiting for him to answer.

And then TNT called out, In here.

Everything seemed to move in slow motion as I followed the
sound of his voice. I found him standing in the middle of an
empty room, staring at a blank wall. In the corner of the room
was a foam mattress, covered with a threadbare sheet that had
probably once been white but had now turned a dark shade of
grey.

I followed the direction of his headlamp. And there, scrawled
on the wall in black permanent marker, was the Roman numeral *I*.

On the wall beside it, also empty, the Roman numeral *II*.

I spun around, reading the remaining walls in a blur: *III*,
IV.

There were no words — no words at all. Just blank walls with
Roman numerals dividing them. Nothing. I stepped outside
the room, hoping to find something else, something more.

In an adjoining room, I found *V*, *VI*, *VII*, *VIII* — but again,
nothing. Nothing except for the numerals, one through ten,
taking up walls, rooms of their own. Talking, to the silence, for
years. Wall after wall: blank. *IX* and *X*, all empty, wordless. I went
back to find TNT.

This is The Ten? I whispered out into the room, my voice
hot in my throat.

I couldn't believe it. It had to be a joke. How could this be The Ten? The legend that I had heard for so long? I ran my fingers along the paint, tracing the curve of the wall, holding my ear to it, listening, hoping that if The Ten were underneath, I could hear Story tell me what they said, say the words.

I can't believe it, TNT said.

Something like *I know* was all I could mutter to him in reply. That this couldn't be The Ten. That it looked like nothing else Story had ever done.

I turned my face to the wall, leaning into it, pressing my cheek hard against it.

TNT confessed that he didn't know that it was going to be like this. That he had hoped to find something extraordinary, too. That he didn't expect to see that there would be nothing. That he was sorry.

All around us, the house was small and dark and quiet.

There's nothing here, I said. Nothing.

I tried to stifle the sobs coming out of my chest but I couldn't. I didn't know what to believe, just that I wanted to believe in something. The Ten. This place. Her. I so wanted it to be real.

I choked back tears. I couldn't believe it was all a lie. Why?

TNT stepped forward and pressed his body against my back, covering me: covering my hand with his hands, pressing his fingertips over mine, burying his head in the small of my neck. His smell filled the small space of air around me. I could feel the heat coming from his body as it touched mine. I wanted to push him away but couldn't. I didn't know anymore what I was supposed to do. Or not do.

He pulled my arms in and turned me around so that my back was against the wall. Then he leaned into me and pressed himself hard against me. And told me to tell him to stop. Because if I didn't he wouldn't be able to stop himself from kissing me. He wanted me. To tell him. To please. Stop.

Say it, he said, his voice like he was in pain. Please.

My heart pounded, skittish and erratic, in the wall of my ribcage like a weird clock.

I can't do that, I said. Because I didn't want to stop. Him or me. From doing anything we wanted.

I leaned forward and kissed him. Our mouths one mouth with no question or hesitation. As he pushed me against the wall, lifting my shirt, undoing his pants, all our movements were fast and clumsy and awkward, as if we'd never touched anyone ever before. As if we'd forgotten how. As if we didn't know what we wanted to do, or how to do it, but found ourselves unable to stop.

XLVII.

It was just after dawn when Thom awoke. He could tell by the colour of the light. It had a pale, fresh look to it, like it was brand new, born out of darkness. He studied the way it streamed through an open window, in soft, broken rays on the wall.

Once again, Thom didn't know where he was. He wasn't at the Ryder. Above him was a large water stain, the ceiling cracked and broken. But he didn't feel as panicked as he usually did. He felt calm and relaxed. Strong. Focused. In a way he had not felt in a long time.

Outside, he could hear the wind in the trees. A cool breeze, the first he had felt in weeks, blew across him. He closed his eyes and smelled the freshness of the air.

Beside him, someone stirred. He turned his head and looked. Aura.

And then he remembered. Everything. How they had made

love and crashed here, on the mattress. Here, on the top of Tiger Mountain.

Aura was still sleeping. Dreaming of something. Lying on her back, her head tilted toward him, her arms resting on her stomach. He studied the dip in her neck where he could see the pulse of her heartbeat, and the way her lips, slightly parted, took in air, her lungs slowly rising and falling. Her hands were so small.

Thom knew he had to tell her who he was. He couldn't hide anymore. From her, from himself, from anyone.

He watched the sun ebb over her shoulder, in waves of dappled leaf-light, tinting her skin gold. As the sun moved across her face, her eyes slowly fluttered open. She looked at him and smiled.

Thom stared into her eyes. He felt like he never wanted to stop looking into them.

She yawned, stretching like a cat in the sun.

I was dreaming, she said. Of Story.

Oh? Thom said.

It's the same dream I always have. There's this train, well, the sound of a train, and as soon as I hear it, I know she's going to show up to tell me where The Ten are. And then she shows me, but I can't see them. Aura paused. I could never see them.

Thom said nothing, only listened.

And then I'd hear the sound of the train again and I'd know she'd go away, leaving me. Last night, I dreamt she didn't leave me. That she was right here, in this room, with me.

Did she show you The Ten?

Aura looked up at the ceiling. Yes.

And what was it like?

It was these walls. These exact same walls. They were empty, just like these are. Then she showed me a new way of looking. And asked if I could see them.

And could you?

Aura stood up from the mattress and moved toward the wall. At the top of it was the single Roman numeral *X*.

Thom stared at Aura as she stood before the wall, watching her watch the faded field of sea-green wall dance with sunlight and shadow, like an abstract painting that had come to life.

Yes, she said. Yes, I can. I never thought anything could be so beautiful.

Me, neither, Thom said, staring at her.

Aura turned around and looked at him.

Why do you think she did it? Or didn't?

Did what?

This, Aura said. Why this, why here? Why Tiger Mountain?

Maybe she needed somewhere to go, Thom said. Away from her family, the G7 —

But why?

Thom remembered standing with Driscoll on the shoreline. What exactly had he meant when he said he knew Story?

Aura came back to the mattress and flopped down beside Thom, pressing against him.

Thom traced his finger along a black wing of her tattoo. When did you get this? he asked.

On my birthday last year. I saved up all my money and got it done. As a gift to myself. As something I could remember I'd done when I was young.

Were you afraid? Thom asked.

Aura looked him in the eye.

Of course. That's why I did it. So that I'd know I wasn't afraid of anything — that I didn't have to be. Then. Now. Or in the future. That if I could stand that kind of pain, I could do anything.

She paused.

My parents don't even acknowledge it. They pretend like it

doesn't even exist. I guess if they think it's not there, then it's really not there. That way they don't have to deal with it, you know? She paused again. Like me, I guess.

You really think that's how they feel? Thom said.

I don't care how they feel, Aura answered with a smile. But you want to know what I really think? Aura said. I think you know way more about me than I know about you.

How about it, TNT? Aura cooed. What deep, dark secret do you wanna share? Cuz I know you got 'em.

She pushed him on his back and straddled him, kissing him, filling his mouth with her tongue, with the sweetness of her lips, taking away all the words he never wanted to say but that he would have to tell her. He had to tell her.

Thom drew his mouth away and gently pushed her away.

Aura, I have to tell you something, Thom said.

What is it? she said.

I, Thom started, I —

He stopped and looked her in the eye.

My real name is Thom. Thomas. I'm a writer who's been working with the police to crack the G7. When I haven't been doing that, I've been living at the Ryder, working with the Graffpol, buffing.

Aura's face went blank.

But I haven't been called by that name in years. I've only ever been known by my tags. Thom paused. That's all I ever wanted to be known by.

The words spilled out of him.

Three months ago I got caught by the cops, Thom continued. Well, I've been caught several times. I've been on the street since I was fifteen, after I ran away from home. This was my shot at a clean record. Not that I ever had any choice. I never wanted to do any of this.

He looked at Aura. She still couldn't say anything.

In the beginning, I thought I would just do what I had to do and get out. And then I met you. And got caught up in the G7. And wanting to know more about Story. Tiger Mountain. The Ten. I couldn't stop. And I couldn't stop wanting to be with you.

He paused and reached out for her.

Don't, Aura said, recoiling from him. Just don't —

I never wanted to hurt you, Thom pleaded. Please believe me.

There was an unbearable silence.

I suppose you know all about me, Aura said. My real name. Where I live. Everything.

It's not like that, Thom said. Please —

Well, then, what is it like? Aura demanded. Chef was right. You're a rat. He said you were gonna burn us all —

Would you forget about Chef and listen to me? Thom said. I'm trying to tell you the truth.

And what truth is that? Aura cried, standing up, tears streaming down her cheeks. About how you're breaking my heart into a million fucking pieces right now? I can't believe you're telling me this — here — now!

Listen. You don't understand. It's about Story, Thom confessed. It's *all* about Story. She's his daughter —

Whose daughter? Aura stuttered, confused.

The cop who sent me here, Thom said. O'Brien. It was all a set-up. He doesn't really care about the G7. He was just using me to find out information.

For what? Getting the G7 busted?

No, Thom said in anger, for finding out about *her*. That was my ticket for getting out. That's why I've been doing this all along —

And what about me? Was I just something you'd been doing all along?

No, never. I, I — Thom struggled to find the words within himself; the words he wanted to say — I wanted to tell you. His voice became very quiet. But I ... I just couldn't —

So you just used me? After everything that's happened! To think I trusted you! That I trusted anybody!

Aura stared at him in disbelief, as she pushed past him and ran out the door, sobbing.

XLVIII.

I stormed out of the house on Tiger Mountain in manic rage. Suffocating. Blinded by tears. Fuck I hate TNT. Those four words repeating, like a mantra in my head: Fuck I hate TNT, Fuck I hate TNT, Fuck I hate TNT, over and over again. My face dripping with sweat. Branches scraping my legs. Running through the trees. Not even seeing where I was going. Not even caring. But just running, running, running, far, far away.

I didn't even know or care about how I was going to get across the river. I just walked right in, getting soaked to the bone. After such a perfect night, I felt like TNT — or Thom, as he called himself — had poisoned my happiness. Infected me with his lies. His treachery. I just wanted to be clean, baptized by the water of the river.

I thought about going home. But I knew there was no way my parents were going to believe my usual story about sleeping over at MC Lee's house. Not with the way I looked. They would know it was bullshit, and I'd have to explain myself. And I didn't feel like explaining myself. I needed somewhere to go.

I decided to go to the Ridgeway. It was, after all, the closest place. And it was still early. No one would be at the clubhouse yet and I could get cleaned up. Eat. And as soon as Mab got there, I could tell her I was sick.

Which I was.

Sick for falling in love with a boy that came to me in a dream.

Sick for thinking that me and him could have been the new king and queen of the scene.

Sick for feeling that I am never going to put the million little shattered pieces of my heart back together again.

Sick of his lies because I can't believe that he did that to me. Me. Aura. Cool girl. Numero Uno. Da shit. The sweetest kiss he is ever going to have in his pathetic life.

Sick for knowing we were destined to be together, even though the entire universe seems to have given me no choice but to hate him, which makes me feel sick even more.

Sick knowing that we shared such an amazing night together and that it will never happen again.

Sick knowing that I have to harbour this secret about him.

Sick knowing that I still love him.

O sick, sick, sick.

Luckily, Queen Mab believes me when I tell her I have to go home because I'm not feeling well. She looks at me all concerned and says, why, yes, yes, of course, your aura doesn't look right, go home. I heave a silent sigh of relief, looking forward to having a good cry alone at home in my bedroom. But as I head out the back kitchen door, The DC is standing there, leaning against the wall. He smiles at me smugly.

I see you got lucky, he says cryptically.

I stare boldly at The DC and tell him I don't know what the fuck he's talking about.

Then he tells me how he saw me come into the Ridgeway early this morning. Very early. He said I probably didn't notice, but he was on the other side of the fence, on the fairway, near the third green, playing a few holes with Kane. Not soon after, he said he saw TNT coming from the same direction. Out of the woods.

My face flushes hot with guilt. You saw nothing, I say.

Then The DC tells me that TNT is a Ryder. And that after they saw him this morning, he and Kane followed him, right up to the front door.

So what, I say. So what if he's a Ryder. That doesn't mean anything. I remind him that he was the one who brought TNT into our fold in the first place.

The DC's mouth curls into a sneer. It doesn't matter. He tells me he's got enough evidence to go to Chef and tell him everything. Unless we can work something out. Just between us. No one would have to know. It would be just like it was before: Aura and The DC.

He reaches out for my waist, pulling me toward him.

Fuck you, I reply.

The DC looks at me and smiles. I try.

At that moment, Queen Mab walks in on us. The DC releases me instantly.

I just got a message from Chef, she says to me. He's coming here. To see *you*.

I glare at The DC, but he only shrugs his shoulders like he knows nothing.

Did he say what it was about? I ask Mab, swallowing the lump of fear in my throat.

No, she continues, glaring at me suspiciously. Only that you should meet him at the gates. Alone. As soon as you can get there.

XLIX.

It took less time than Thom thought to get back to the Ryder.

And Thom, perhaps for the first time, could hardly wait to see Driscoll. Because he was going to ask him every question he could — about the G7, Chef BS, Story, everyone.

Even Aura. Despite what had happened, he knew deep in his heart he had done the right thing when he had told her the truth about who he was.

On his way through the back door, he ran into Omar.

Yo, bro, Omar said to Thom with a fist bump. Wassup?

Thom played it cool.

Not much. You know. The usual Graffpol shit. Cruising Buff City with Captain D.

Omar's face slid into a suspicious smile. Didn't you hear? Driscoll's gone.

What?

Yeah, first thing I heard this morning. Driscoll's been fired or some shit.

Where did he go?

Omar shrugged. Dunno, man. All I heard was him and Winston getting into a big fight. They were shouting at each other in Winston's office. I heard the whole thing. Saw Driscoll leaving, slamming the door and shit. Then that was it. Nothin'. And Driscoll's been MIA ever since.

When did this happen? Thom asked.

Last night.

Thom panicked. Something strange was going down. None of it made any sense. Driscoll had been Thom's only real connection to anything. Even if he was an asshole, he was the only asshole Thom could really trust.

Hey, man, Omar said to Thom. You okay?

Thom looked at Omar in a daze. What? Me? Oh, yeah, sure. And then without saying another word, he began walking down the hall to Winston's office. Thom wasn't sure what he was going to say, but he had to talk to someone. He stood before Winston's door and knocked loudly.

Come in, he heard Winston say from the other side.

As Thom opened the door, Winston was sitting at his desk, in front of his computer.

I need to talk to you, Thom said. Now.

Winston looked up at Thom cautiously. I don't know if I have any time this morning —

I need to talk to you, Thom repeated. Now. It's about Driscoll.

Winston raised an eyebrow. Yes?

Where is he? Omar told me he's been fired.

Winston lowered his arms and crossed them against his chest. Yes. Driscoll's been fired. For drinking on the job. I'm sure you can understand how unacceptable this kind of situation is —

Hire him back, Thom said. Driscoll led me to some really important places. And I was really close to finding out some important information, Thom confessed.

Winston said nothing. The room was heavy with silence.

He was becoming a liability, Winston said. I'd warned him before. The drinking had to stop. In the end, I simply had no choice.

I know the drinking was bad, Thom said. But you can't fire him. I need him —

Winston narrowed his eyes and looked flatly at Thom.

For what?

To find out about the G7. Thom paused. For the investigation. My agreement with O'Brien —

I know what your agreement with O'Brien was, interrupted Winston. His voice was terse and quiet. Do you know what I am? I am, above all other things, an administrator. Which means that I administer the programs and services for the youth that I am responsible for. Which includes, whether you like or not, *you*. You may have struck a deal with O'Brien, but I am responsible for you. And you will abide by the rules of the Ryder while you are under my roof. It's a roof that's served this community for more than twenty years, that's provided hope and meaning to hundreds of youths. I won't have the Ryder be jeopardized as an institution just because of one individual. Or one investigation.

Thom couldn't believe what he'd just heard. What the fuck is that supposed to mean?

It means, Winston replied slowly, that I have accurately assessed every angle of the situation and executed a strategy to address all the possible outcomes.

All of a sudden Thom remembered that O'Brien had told him not to mention anything to Winston.

I don't have time for this shit. Where's Driscoll? Thom demanded.

I don't know, said Winston, as he looked down at the paperwork on his desk. Now if you'll excuse me, I have to get back to work —

What are you doing? Thom yelled.

My job, Winston said. And I'll remind you to keep your voice down, because whether you like it or not you are in a correctional facility. Which is why, no matter what agreement you and O'Brien have, I'll remind you that I am the only one, by law, who has the supervisory authority to sign your release papers. Perhaps O'Brien failed to mention that. I'm sure he failed to mention a lot of things.

Are you threatening me? Thom said.

Winston said nothing.

This is bullshit, Thom exclaimed. All this fucking double-speak.

Winston sat smugly in his chair, surrounded by his pictures of the highest peaks in the world, weighed in by his papers and his work, his responsibilities, while deceiving his Ryders with the illusion, the false promise, of conquering mountains — without ever letting them leave or giving them their freedom. Rage, hot and thick, filled Thom's throat.

Which of these mountains have you climbed, huh? Thom shot at Winston. You've never climbed any of them, have you? You just sit there, in your fucking administrator's chair, exploring the top of the world from your fucking laptop. Your world is flat. You've never climbed Denali, Thom scoffed as he stared down at the chunk of mountain rock on the floor, his voice filled with disgust. You've never even been there. Have you? *Have you?*

Winston was silent.

I'll be sure to review your recommendations and include them in my assessment of your rehabilitation and final report, Winston said finally as looked back at his computer screen. Good day.

Thom stormed out of Winston's office and ran down the hallway, ripping down every mountain poster that he could. He knew exactly what he had to do. He went straight to his room and stuffed his clothes into the bottom of his backpack, dragging out the bag of graff gear from under his bed.

He had so little. He always had. The streets, his walls: his writing had always been all he had ever needed.

On his way out, Thom stopped and took one last look at Tariq, Duke, and Ray in the kitchen, joking with Jeremy, their boisterous voices rising in discordant harmony. Sitting at the table, Carlos was buried in a book, reading. Only Omar met his gaze, studying him carefully. The two exchanged knowing glances, nodding at each other respectfully. Somehow, he had earned that respect. Just by being one of them, being a Ryder. It wasn't something he felt he deserved. But something he had felt honoured to be. Thom dropped the bag of graff supplies in the corner of the room and turned around and started walking down the hallway.

You going to work? Ray yelled at his back.

Thom nodded.

You know the rule — Ray started.

Stay cool, Thom finished.

He heard them call out with shouts of praise and laughter. Then he heard Omar yell that he had forgotten his bag.

But Thom just kept walking. He couldn't look back now.

As he ran out the back door of the Ryder, Thom stood at the edge of the parking lot and saw Driscoll's truck parked in the corner, vibrating with the booming pulse of bass.

Thom ran across the asphalt to where the passenger door was swung open, waiting.

Get in, Driscoll said, not looking at him above the pounding beat. Now. There's something I need to tell you. Something you need to know.

L.

I made my way down the long, winding driveway to the gates, my heart pounding. It was totally unusual for Chef to come to the Ridgeway. He refused to step foot on the grounds on account of the fact that he believed golf courses were elitist, environmental nightmares. His coming to meet me meant something was serious. Very serious.

It didn't take long for Kierkegaard to find me. He came

familiarly trotting toward me, nudging his wet black nose into
my hand. Could he smell my fear? Know where I was? Where I
had been? Who I had been with?

As I walked through the gates with Kierkegaard close by my
side, Chef BS was standing in a circle of shade under a tree,
waiting for me. I felt him looking at me, staring.

Comrade Aura, he said as I came closer, how lovely to see
you. I'm so glad you're here.

I could hardly breathe my heart was pounding so bad. He
stepped forward and leaned over and whispered in my ear:

I've come here to see you about a mountain, he said softly.
I think you know the one I mean. His lips brushed my ear. I
want you to take me there. Now.

As I led Chef through the trees, I felt his eye on my back,
burning through me, like a magnifying glass angled to the
sun. I thought about running, but there was no way I was
going to escape Kierkegaard, who stayed close to us at every
step. I had no choice but to take Chef to Tiger Mountain. To make
him see. Show him everything.

Chef was silent the entire way. I felt sick. Through my
stupidity and ignorance, I had betrayed the G7, but I couldn't
bring myself to offer Chef my confession. My own shame
choked me, like mud in my throat.

As we crossed the river and made our way up the path, I
thought of how I would see the same room where TNT and
I had been together. Where The Ten were. Their meaning hit
me again and I thought of how Story must have felt escaping
into these woods. Renegade. Free. Breaking loose of everything,
even writing. TNT's words echoed in me. Considering who
she was, it was now obvious to me why Story would have
come here. What was she running away from. I wondered if

Chef knew and had kept the truth of her identity from us, too.

As I approached the front door of the house, I wondered when TNT had left. And how he had felt, after. And if he had longed, even for a second, to come and find me. To call out for me through the trees. To say he was sorry. To tell me more about who he was and what happened. Because I couldn't stop thinking about him now that I was here again. Now that he was gone.

I watched Kierkegaard sniff madly around the outside of the house. I was about to open the door, when Chef pushed past me and walked straight in. I followed behind him quietly. In the full light of day, Story's empty walls sang out in their strange sea-green colour, resembling a faded turquoise, the colour of tropical water. Chef's eye drifted stonily toward the bed, then at me.

He laughed softly to himself. I was confused. If he knew anything about what had happened between me and TNT, he wasn't saying. But why was he laughing? None of how he was behaving made any sense.

I am eternally grateful, he announced to me, for you have led me to the truth.

What truth? I said.

Chef lifted his arms and spun around, slow and languorous, through the pale, aqueous air as if he were drowning in the middle of the room.

This, he said. *This truth*.

What are you talking about?

He stopped and fell to his knees before Story's empty walls. *This*, he said.

I still didn't understand. He didn't care about TNT, or me, at all. It was all about her. Story. Could he really have not known where The Ten were, all this time? How was that possible?

I thought you knew, I said to him. That you had always known. But had just chosen to keep it secret. To protect her.

Chef laughed again. But this time it was a sad, bitter laughter.

No, he said. Not this. I never knew where this was. I only ever suspected. And now I have the proof.

Then he told me how Story liked to keep secrets. About herself. Others. How she collected them, like they were jewels. Some were hard, impenetrable. Some she shared. But not this one. Not this secret. This was one he never knew.

I stood, motionless, listening. Staring at Chef. He was unshaven, unwashed, dark circles ringed under his eyes; his mane of hair tousled and unkempt. Dirty. He looked like he hadn't slept in days. Not since the last time I saw him at the Library.

Chef pulled himself up and ran his fingers along the wall, touching its surface as if it were skin. Riveted, I stood there, watching him.

Story never did anything without thinking of its full meaning, Chef said. Which is why she only ever worked with text. Words and phrases. She wanted words to weigh in people's minds in unusual ways. For people to hear her voice. To listen to what she had to say.

He remembered meeting her at a house party. How they had connected instantly. Talked all night. Afterwards, when everyone else had left, they went outside and lay together on the grass. Just before dawn, she fell asleep in his arms. It was very fine and rare, he said. And he remembered lying there, holding her, and that it felt like he was holding a ray of light in his arms. Something hard and bright and true. And once he saw it, it was the most exceptional thing. As if Story had given him the gift of sight. So he could see, finally, everything. Only one other person had ever made him feel that way. And Story reminded him of her.

Chef turned around and faced me.

The same way that you remind me of Story.

I bowed my head and laughed nervously. Because now I was really confused. First, there was the ear brush with the lips. Then this. I tried to think of something to say but all I really wanted was to get the fuck out of there. What was going on? Chef was really creeping me out.

Why would Story hide The Ten? I asked him, trying to change the subject. What was she trying to protect?

Because, Chef told me, she wanted to own it for herself. To keep it from me, from the G7. Because she wanted, ultimately, to be free. From me; from everything. The Ten was her send-off.

What, like a suicide note? I said. But I thought you were with her when she —

Died? No. Chef turned his face away. I was never there. Though I should have been.

Suddenly, the room was no longer filled with light, and I realized the sun had passed over us. The room was just as it had been when TNT and I first found it: empty, dirty. The walls scrawled with empty prophecy.

Story did it to hurt me, Chef continued. To get back at me. I never thought she could love anyone else. Of course I suspected it. The pain of sadness rose in his voice. But now I know.

I felt like the air was being sucked out of me. I stared at the bed in the corner of the room. The empty walls. Story had come here, hid here, slept here. But with who? I realized then that maybe Story didn't die over one lover or another but because she was torn between loving two of them.

I thought of TNT. What would happen to him now? I ached with the thought of never seeing him again. I didn't care who he was. I wanted to be with him. For us to be together. Outside,

I could hear a nearby train. I couldn't lose TNT like Chef had lost Story. I needed to find him. Talk to him. Tell him it wasn't too late — for us. Yet.

But all of that didn't really matter now, Chef said. He didn't care. What happened with her. Or him. Because both of them had gotten what they deserved. And we were alone. Him and I, together, now. Which he thought was rather fateful somehow. Considering everything.

Chef BS reached out and gently stroked my shoulder with his hand. His touch was hypnotic, electrifying. Like a line of fire being drawn over my skin. And scary as hell.

I stepped back.

If Chef didn't know where The Ten were, how did he know I knew where they were? Had The DC told him? TNT? Who? I didn't know how he knew, but somehow he knew. *He knew.*

Chef asked innocently, What? What are you afraid of?

How did you know to ask me to bring you here, knowing I had been here before?

Chef ignored me. I have something important to tell you.

I want you to take over the G7, he said. Be the creative director, so to speak. You won't have to shadow anyone ever again. Especially TNT. That was just, as I said, a test. To prove what I already knew.

I was shocked. You knew TNT was a rat?

He told you? Chef smirked. I didn't expect him to have so much moral character. Chef paused arrogantly. Of course I knew. From the first time I saw him.

But how? And if you knew, why did you involve him in what we were doing? Choose me?

Because I needed him, Chef said. To settle an old debt. Though he didn't know that was what he was doing. Not that it matters now. It's done.

I couldn't believe I had been used, like TNT, as a pawn in Chef's game.

I don't want to work on the streets anymore, Chef said. I've had my moment. Now it's up to you. I knew from the first time I saw your work that you could take the G7 into the future. I will still shadow you, of course, he said gently, until you're ready. You still have much to learn.

Then he touched me again and I wondered what that meant, exactly. But I said nothing.

At last Kierkegaard came into the room and wedged himself between us. I stepped back against the wall as Chef bent down and stroked Kierkegaard's fur in long, hard strokes.

He knows she was here, he said. He recognizes her smell. Chef looked into the empty room, his hardened gaze returning to the bed in the corner. The physical traces of her are invisible to us, but for him, they're everywhere.

For a moment the ghost of whatever or whoever Story had been for him flowed through the room and shimmered between us, like a thin, radiant mist.

Chef raised his face to look at me. He was, I finally understood, possessed. *Haunted.* Don't you see? His eyes were gleaming. It's *her*, he said rhapsodically.

Then I realized that although he was looking directly at me, he wasn't looking at *me*. He never had been. He had only ever seen me as a substitute for Story; a memory made somehow visible.

He stood up.

I know I've given you a lot to think about. But if you lead the G7 you could create a whole other universe of possibility.

But what about TNT? I asked, trying to hide the desperation in my voice.

Chef laughed lightly and lit a cigarette.

Don't worry about him. He'll be taken care of. My old friend Winston has a plan for him.

LI.

Thom stared at Driscoll's profile in the truck as they spun out of the Ryder's parking lot. It was hard to believe he had spent so much time working with someone only to realize he knew absolutely nothing about him.

Who are you? Thom asked.

Driscoll forced a dark smile and looked at Thom. I might ask you the same question. You tell me.

I don't know, Thom muttered, looking away, confused. I don't know anything anymore.

Outside the window of the truck, the city flitted past before his vision, window frame by window frame. He had only ever really known it by night: the secret language of its territories, its walls and alleyways. During the day he had only been a slave to its erasure, eradicating any possible expression.

What happened? Thom asked Driscoll. Why did Winston fire you?

Winston's got a grudge against me, Driscoll grimaced. He doesn't trust me. And he's scared. Of what I might say. Of what I might do. Driscoll paused. Of what I might tell someone like you.

Someone like you. The words hung, leaden with resentment, in the air.

What's that supposed to mean?

You're a rat, Driscoll said. I could smell it on you from the first day you came on crew.

Thom looked awkwardly down at his hands. It wasn't by choice, he said, defending himself. Believe me.

It never is, Driscoll said.

Thom wondered what he meant by that. Where are you taking me?

You'll see. Did you find Tiger Mountain? Driscoll asked him.

Yes, Thom said. And The Ten.

Alone?

No. Thom paused. With another writer. Aura —

Aura? No way. I've buffed her! Many times. He laughed darkly. Thom thought about telling him about what had happened between him and Aura. But he still wasn't sure if he could trust Driscoll completely.

Why are you doing this?

What? Saving your sorry ass?

Yeah.

Because no one ever did it for me, Driscoll said, his voice full of hate.

Thom stared at Driscoll. What happened to you?

Driscoll turned and stared at him, then looked away. The same thing that happened to you. I just got caught. That's all.

But there's more to it than that, isn't there? Thom said angrily. Look, why don't you stop your bullshit and tell me the truth?

You want the truth?

Driscoll veered into an empty parking lot on the edge of a rail yard. Multiple train tracks unfolded before them in a parallel grid of steel lines. Near the rear tracks Thom saw some decommissioned, abandoned rail cars: all of them were covered with graffiti.

Driscoll turned off the engine and reached for his canteen. Thom had never known the truck to be so quiet. A rare and pure silence filled the space between them.

I first met Story through BS, Driscoll began, after we both

got out of the Ryder. He and I had been there at the same time, and did the same time, together. We were always getting into trouble. Doing shit we shouldn't have done but did anyway just because we knew we could and didn't care. And even though he knew we were shit disturbers, Winston loved us anyway. Gave us mountain names.

Which is why you're Everest, Thom said. But what about Chef BS?

Winston named him that because his first name was Blake —

Like the poet, Thom said, making the connection.

Yes, Driscoll said, and because his last name was Starfield. It got shortened to Chef BS pretty quick when he started dishing up these stories about how he was reborn in outer space after growing up on these hardcore meds and having this twisted foster home past. Apparently when he was just thirteen, Chef "died," faking his own death to get out of the foster home he was living in. I guess his foster father had beat him up so bad he had detached his retina. Which is why he said he only had one eye. But it didn't matter. BS just stuck, and Winston felt sorry for him. Loved him, like a son. Chef could do no wrong.

But Winston said none of the G7 ever stayed at the Ryder, Thom said.

Driscoll took a long drink from his stainless steel water container, which Thom knew didn't contain any water.

Technically we never became the G7 until *after* we left the Ryder, Driscoll clarified. So, in a sense, what Winston told you was the truth. Bastard.

He paused.

When I first met Story, I didn't even like her. And she didn't like me at all. She was totally in awe of Chef. Chef this, Chef that. She worshipped him. Like he was some kind of genius or something. Which he was. But once we started working to-gether, something happened. I don't know what it was, exactly. It was like we could talk to each other through our writing. Have it speak for us. Say the words we couldn't say.

Thom thought of how he and Aura had done the same. How they had used their writing as a way to define themselves, to show others how they wanted to be seen, to be read. To be understood.

By then Chef started to notice it, too, Driscoll went on, though Story and I hadn't done anything. Yet. When he first formed the G7, Chef started making all these critical demands, telling us what we should and shouldn't do, telling us what was and wasn't art, and he and Story got into this big fight because she didn't want to feel like he was controlling her. And then later that night we went out, together, just the two of us. We went swimming. Discovered the Kalpa Path. Tiger Mountain. And things just happened.

Thom thought of last night and the time he had spent with Aura. How could he have let her go? Why hadn't he run after her, telling her how sorry he was, how he hated himself for do-ing what he had done but that he had no choice and wanted nothing but to be with her?

So she's the tiger, Thom said slowly, piecing it together. And you're the mountain. And the flames?

You know that saying that writers have when their writing is still up? That it's burning?

Thom nodded.

The flames are proof that we're still burning. Out there. Up there. With the will to live, to love, to write, to be free. Even when we're long gone from the scene. We'll still be up there, burning from the inside, up on Tiger Mountain.

A train was moving into the yard. Thom stared at its speeding square bulk as it blurred past. Thom wondered if Driscoll knew Story was O'Brien's daughter.

Meanwhile, Driscoll said, there was this big crackdown going on in the city against graffiti. You know, the city administration passing bylaws and all that shit to put a band-aid solution on an urban development crisis they don't have the infrastructure, vision, services or tax basis to solve; appeasing business owners by putting the heat on the cops to bust latchkey kids who have nowhere to go but gravitate to downtown and decide to get high and get up with a can of spray they racked from some hardware store? Driscoll sighed deeply. Such bullshit. Of course, the G7, being so visible, was a major target. All of us were. Me, Chef, and Story. Though she was the first to get caught.

Thom thought about how the news of that would have gone down in the O'Brien household. He recalled the pictures on O'Brien's desk and thought of them as real people, assembled around a dinner table together, fighting.

When I found out that Story got caught, Driscoll continued, I went fucking crazy. I couldn't bear the thought of her being locked up. So I went to Winston and made a deal with him to give myself up. For her. So she could be free. It wasn't until after I'd given myself up I learned that Chef had already made a deal with Winston, tipping him off about Story.

Chef BS turned Story in? Thom was shocked. But why?

Because Chef suspected something was going on between me and Story. And he was jealous. He wanted to punish us. But he never thought I'd give myself up. Or that I'd become Big Brother, Captain D of the Graffpol. I never waged war against graffiti, Driscoll declared, I only waged war against Chef. For what he did. To her. He paused. To me. To us.

Driscoll stopped talking and watched the train roll past. Names of writers from all over the country and the continent

appeared on every car. Big, small; it didn't matter what size.
The cars rolled past: steel canvasses bombed, burned, tagged.

It'll never stop, Driscoll said. This is what the cops don't
understand. That no matter what happens, there's *always* going
to be someone who's going to do *that* —

Driscoll pointed at a boxcar, painted with a roller, covered
in its entirety in white paint with the word *DEUS*. For a brief
second, the letters filled the landscape, transcending space and
time, giving new power to the word, offering a new meaning, a
new identity.

They watched it roll by in a grave, honoured silence.

Why are you telling me all this? Thom said.

Because I want you to go tell whoever it is you're working for
what a fraud Winston is. That he's been protecting Chef and
the G7 for years. And the cops need to know the truth. About
everything. I can't do it. But you can. Driscoll looked at him
and smiled. You know how it is: they won't believe a word from
an asshole like me.

Thom laughed quietly, shaking his head. It was so true.

For once, there was a moment of comfortable silence between
them.

But what about the Ten? Thom asked.

What about them? Driscoll asked.

Well, what do they mean?

Whatever you want them to, whatever you need them to be.
At least that's what Story said to me.

Thom needed to find Aura. Tell her everything, again. Find a
way for them to be together again. He had to make her believe.
That what he felt for her was real.

In the rail yard, a few men were walking up and down the
tracks with clipboards, inspecting small boxes on the lines.

How long do you think we have before we get caught? Thom

wondered out loud. Winston's probably already called the cops on us.

He wouldn't do that, Driscoll said. We have too much on him. He's hoping we'll run.

Why didn't you tell me all this sooner?

Because I needed to know I could trust you. That you would know and believe the truth — the real truth — when you heard it.

Driscoll took another sip from his canteen.

What will you do now? Thom asked.

Oh, I don't know. I've done my duty here, Driscoll said as he turned on the ignition. Besides, I got somewhere I've been meaning to go for a long time, somewhere where someone's waiting for me.

Where?

On the stereo, Thom recognized Led Zeppelin's "Misty Mountain Hop." But Driscoll said nothing, and just smiled at him.

LII.

That afternoon, I came down Tiger Mountain alone, since Chef told me he wanted to stay up there by himself and think some things through. I walked back the whole way, trying to understand what had happened. Between TNT's confession, The DC's threats, and Chef's request, I felt totally unbalanced and needed to find some solid ground to stand on. So I went home.

At first I was really scared, since I knew I would probably get into some serious shit when I walked in the door. Which I was kind of hoping for. Some jarring, grounding reality that would affix me to the spot. My mom would look up at me and ask me where I'd been. Then maybe she'd even get mad at me. Even pretend to care. Make me clean my room. Take out the trash. Whatever normal parents do.

But, alas, no one was there. I mean, really. How could they just be gone? How, I asked myself, was it possible that I could be so invisible to them? Didn't they even know I'd been gone? Or care? How was it possible in all this time that I'd been bombing the city upside down that they had gone and become zombies like everyone else?

Deflated, I went up to my room. When I walked in the door, the evidence of my double life slapped me in the face. I stared at my prim, white canopy bed. The quaint bookshelf. The painted white desk. The modest wardrobe, hiding between closed doors.

It was no wonder my parents didn't worry about me. Why they didn't care. Obviously, they saw this and thought that their daughter was perfectly happy, that she was a zombie, too.

I threw my SOL backpack on my bed and pulled everything out, studying its inventory. Headlamp. Coffee mug. Money. Black book. My dugout pipe. Pen. Gum. Lip gloss. Can of spray paint. I picked up the can and shook it, considering what it might be like to bomb my room. That would certainly get my parents' attention. But then again I didn't want to end up sitting in some dumbass psychologist's chair, expressing my feelings about my remorse and how fucked up my parents truly were.

I mean, seriously. Really.

I flopped back on my bed and stared up at the ceiling, considering what it would be to be head of the G7; thinking of all the projects I could do, what I could get away with. If only I didn't have to *do* Chef to do it. Or whatever else he wanted me for. Anger spiked all over me again, thinking of everything he had said. I was saddened and disappointed. I had always been so in awe of him, of everything he did. Of all he was. The myth and legend he had made me believe he was. Now I couldn't even think of him without feeling sick. I shuddered with revulsion, thinking of how he had touched me.

As I lay there, I fell asleep, and then I had the dream about Story. The one I always have. Except this time, it's different. First of all, Kierkegaard's in it, howling, and I get to the part when Story says *Look back. Don't you see?* I do. And instead of darkness there's a wall covered with graffiti. Layer upon layer of words and paint, unrecognizable. But beautiful. Laden with every colour. Every style. The paint so thick it's 3D, morphing and moving in front of me, like the wall's alive.

I go up to the wall and touch it, and when I do, this tiny crack starts from my fingertip, and it grows, bigger and bigger, with this light pushing through from the other side, and as I step through the wall, into the light, there's a mirror, and when I look into it I see Story is me. *Don't you see?* And then everything explodes, in a big kaboom.

When I wake up, it's early evening. And there's a calm and quiet, like anything is possible. Soft, warm light swims through the air. I get up and look outside my window, over the sea of roof-tops. Into the trees. I see a cloud of smoke in the distance. Reaching up into the sky. From where I know Tiger Mountain is.

A terrible dread and horror fills me. And I think of how Chef told me about Story. How he tried to seduce me. Asked me to lead the G7. And, finally, how he wanted to stay there, alone. I think of my dream, of Kierkegaard howling. Of Story's empty walls. All of them, burning on Tiger Mountain.

And I know I have to go to him, find him.

TNT.

Knowing somehow that he, too, is out there, looking for me. I can just feel it. Like the way I did the first night. When I went to the Bridge.

Intuitively, I know that's where he'll be, where he'll be waiting for me.

I shove some extra clothes into my backpack. A towel. My sketchbook. The last of the weed Kane gave me. More spray and paint markers. And all the money I have stashed away.

It isn't that I don't want to stay and work with the G7. I can't. Not now. They are like the wall in my dream. And TNT is like the light, casting out the darkness, letting me see, and not just who I am, but who I could be.

I know I'm not Story. I am me. I am Aura. And he is TNT. I can't even bring myself to call him by his other name. To even think of him as that. Whoever that is. That isn't who I fell for; that isn't who I know.

The guy I know is a beautiful boy, a writer named TNT.

I look out the window again and watch the sky fill with a dull orange haze, the sun setting like a broken ember against the trees.

I sling my backpack over my shoulders and go downstairs.

I decide I am going to start my life, my real life of the real me, over again. Right here and now.

My parents, who must have arrived while I was sleeping and who are having their pre-dinner cocktail, just look at me and smile as if I never even left. As I wave goodbye and walk out the door, they call my name, but I don't even hear them.

LIII.

After Driscoll dropped him off downtown, Thom seriously considered going to O'Brien's office. But experience had taught him better. If he went there, they could do anything to him they wanted. But he had to tell O'Brien what he knew. So Thom found a payphone and dug out the card with O'Brien's name and number, along with some change Driscoll had given him. He pressed the digits and waited, listening.

O'Brien picked up almost instantly.

Listen, I can't talk long. But I bet you think you've seen me, or kids like me, in the movies, right? So listen up. You'll know exactly how this works.

He could hear O'Brien breathing heavily on the other end of the line.

The first thing I do is tell you that the guy who you think is guilty really isn't. And that the guy you least expect and think is innocent is the guy who really did it.

You're bullshitting, O'Brien said.

No, I'm not, Thom said. Are you listening?

Yeah, O'Brien said.

Good. Go talk to Winston. I think you'll find, once you start digging, he has plenty of information about the G7. What you don't find at the Ryder I'm sure you can find at Io. Or Tiger Mountain. Or the Library. I already gave you those directions. Winston will tell you where everything else is.

Thom didn't have much time. He had to get to the Bridge. Somehow he knew Aura would be there, waiting for him.

His eyes flitted across the street, catching sight of a burner high up on a wall by some new writer he hadn't seen. It was done in wildstyle, in pink and black and yellow and turquoise. The single word, *EXSTATIC*, could be discerned, leaping out of the crevices of the concrete, demanding to be seen, read, heard.

Thom could feel his heart beating inside him, and for the first time in a long time, he wasn't afraid of anything.

Oh, and another thing. Don't try to find me. That's always what they say in the movies, right? When the good kid gets away at the end? Well, that's me. And that's what I'm telling you. So don't even try.

What do you know about my daughter? O'Brien begged, his voice desperate.

Thom thought of his father, his mother. How little they knew about who he was, of how they never wanted to know. No one leaves home unless something's really wrong. Like him, Story had run away for a reason.

Why don't you ask yourself that question? Thom replied.

And then, without another word, Thom hung up and stepped through a crowd of people, and walked toward the Bridge.

LIV.

Just before sunrise, he steps out from the path in the treeline, emerging onto the railroad track. He looks down the line, left to right, noting the gently sloping, grassy sections on either side of the tracks.

She was right. This was a perfect place to catch out.

He bends down on one knee and puts his ear to the track.

Listening. Nothing is coming. Yet.

Last night, he hiked along the river to the farthest point south in the city, snaking his way through a series of inter-connected fields and forests to the place she wrote to him about. In the cool wave of light from his headlamp, he could hardly see where he was going as he walked through the maze of forest. He slept under the trees on a groundsheet, falling asleep to an ocean of cricket sounds. Dreaming of mountains. Her voice. Her eyes.

He can't believe the day has finally arrived.

Soon. Three days. They will be together. Finally, again.

The sun is getting higher. He stares up into the endless blue vista of sky. Not a cloud in sight.

He is dressed in layers of dark clothes to disguise himself

at night and to keep him warm, in case it got cold. In his bag he carries his canteen and some non-perishable food, some gloves and a hat, along with a warm, waterproof jacket. Between the pages of his stolen copy of Hillary's *High Adventure* is a train map and some cash he has been saving.

While he waits, he changes his shoes for his boots and stands up again, looking down the line. In the distance, he can see a small pinpoint of something yellow, flickering, in the distance. A soft wave of hot air blows over his face.

The train is coming.

He stands there, watching the small pinpoint of yellow light getting larger and larger, shimmering in the heat.

He recalls the last morning they spent together. Those two years ago. How there was nothing more to be said. How he remembered holding her and not wanting to let go but knowing he had to. How they had made up their minds to carry out their plan. For justice. For this day.

He reaches into his backpack and puts on his gloves and tightens the straps of his backpack. Then he backs up into the grass, crouches down on his hands and knees, and waits.

Fear grips him. As it approaches, the train moves faster than anything he can remember. Then cars rattle past him at a terrifying speed, shaking the tracks with a strange possession. The sound is deafening.

When he finally sees an open boxcar, he springs up on his legs and sprints alongside the train until he sees a steel handle he can grab on to. He reaches out with his hand and in one fluid motion grabs the handle tightly, pulling his body, legs, and feet up into the empty boxcar, rolling safely inside, collapsing on the steel floor, breathless, his heart pounding.

For a moment he just lies there, feeling the vibrations of the floor under his body, listening to the sound of the train rattle beneath him. When he feels able, he stands up and stares out the open doorway, his legs throbbing with adrenalin, the forests blurring past him.

As the train speeds through a wide, flat field, sunlight floods the car.

He stands in the open doorway and leans against its inner frame, feeling the light shine down on him.

Acknowledgements

Many thanks to Ali McDonald and Sam Hiyate and the staff at The Rights Factory, for supporting my vision; to Barry Jowett and everyone at Cormorant, for believing in the work; to Paul Walde, always, for love and friendship.

Thanks to Andrew Francis, maven extraordinaire, for connecting me with Neil Kellock and his team at The Windermere Manor, and for their support in my residency at the Western Research Park; and to Jackie Garlick-Pynaert, an early reader who offered important feedback.

Special thanks to James Kirkpatrick for the inspiration of his stories and his art.

A big shout out must also go to the landscape and writers of London, Ontario, Canada, without whom this tale could never have been imagined, or told.

I would also like to gratefully acknowledge both the Canada Council for the Arts and the Ontario Arts Council for their support in the creation of this book.